Fury of the .44

Adam Brady

A Black Horse Western

ROBERT HALE

First published by Cleveland Publishing Co. Pty Ltd,
New South Wales, Australia
First published in 1967
© 2019 by Piccadilly Publishing

This edition © The Crowood Press, 2019

ISBN 978-0-7198-3065-5

The Crowood Press
The Stable Block
Crowood Lane
Ramsbury
Marlborough
Wiltshire SN8 2HR

www.bhwesterns.com

Robert Hale is an imprint
of The Crowood Press

Typeset by
Derek Doyle & Associates, Shaw Heath
Printed and bound in Great Britain by
4Bind Ltd, Stevenage, SG1 2XT

ONE

LOOKING FOR REDEMPTION

Buck Halliday tallied up his problems as he rode across the heat-seared, barren country.

He had come through three dust storms in the last five days and was no longer sure if the trail he was following was the shortest route – or even the right route – to Redemption.

His weary horse was weakening with each step it took. He had enough water left for the noon stop. After that, both horse and rider would go thirsty. They were already going hungry. Any scrap of vegetation which might have nourished a horse had frizzled up and blown away weeks ago. Halliday had swallowed his last shaving of jerky that morning. It seemed like that had been hours ago, and so it was, although the horse had carried him no more than ten miles since sunup.

Even so, he decided that he could handle most things that this day in the desert was likely to throw at him. It was just that tomorrow was another story . . . although tomorrow might bring a cactus with some juice in it, or even a waterhole.

Hell, why stop at that? Maybe tomorrow would be the day he would stumble on a running creek full of clear, sweet water and fish with a mind to jump right into the skillet.

He let the sorrel select its own way across a long, gradual slope covered in loose gravel while he walked an hour, rode an hour, with only the clip-clop of the horse's hoofs and the jingle of the bridle to break the silence.

He was so accustomed to seeing and hearing nothing in the crushing desert silence that it took awhile for him to register that he was seeing buzzards. Another one circled and swooped, and then he could hear it grunting and hissing.

When he came closer, he saw that there were about a dozen of them, fighting over the carcass of a dead steer. The devil birds did not leave their prize until Halliday picked up a rock and threw it, and even then, they immediately settled again.

The significance of the dead steer was not lost on him. Not long ago, that critter had been lost and alone without water – and now it was a banquet for buzzards.

He led the horse until the buzzards were out of his sight and hearing, and then a little further he spotted a dry wash and figured the eroded bank might provide a little shade.

He unsaddled the horse and wet his bandanna to moisten the sorrel's mouth. Then he wet his own lips and tongue and tightly stoppered the canteen that had just a few drops left.

'Well, hoss,' he said, 'I'm gonna do my damnedest to sleep until that sun starts to go down. If you're smart, you'll try to do the same.'

As he'd hoped, the bank of the dry wash protected him from the sun if he crawled in close. The ground was as hot as a griddle, though, so he got the saddle blanket and lay down on that.

He was somewhere between torpor and consciousness when his mind registered the distant echo of a gunshot.

He stood up slowly and looked around, shook out the blanket and saddled the horse. He could not see anything until he climbed into the saddle and rode to the top of the bank. There it was – a suspended cloud of dust . . . and another gunshot.

Halliday nursed the sorrel into a fast walk and headed straight for the dust cloud.

Before long, the country fell away in front of him, and down below stood a shabby little settlement. It wasn't much, but if there were people, there had to be water and food.

He counted three shacks with chimneys and a lean-to before he understood what it was all about. The cattle pens and the railroad siding had to be the reason for the shacks – why else would anyone elect to live on this ragged edge of hell?

Could this be Redemption?

Halliday grinned at the double meaning. The dust was coming from the cattle pens, although it was so thick down there that he could scarcely see the milling beasts that were raising it.

None of that explained the gunfire though, he reminded himself as he came slowly down toward the pens. Seven days of heat and dust, thirst and hunger, he wondered just what Redemption would bring. . . .

Now he could see the men – five cowpokes on the outside between him and the pens, four towners eating dust inside the pens. On the siding beyond them, a thin wisp of white smoke drifted occasionally from the smokestack of a freight train.

Halliday drew rein at a decent distance and waited for the men to check him out.

The man in the middle of the bunch outside the pens was short, bearded and aged. He was also scowling and holding a gun. The four who stood around him had their empty hands hovering significantly at their sides.

Halliday removed his hat and swept his hand

through his black, curly hair. He returned the old man's stare and bobbed his head in a greeting that was not returned. Then his eyes swept across the four men in the pen.

His attention settled on the tallest of the quartet, a lean man with a double gun rig, a black town suit and dark eyes which stared back at Halliday from under the brim of a black hat. The bearded old man turned slightly to get a better look at the intruder, and then he snapped;

'Who the hell're you?'

'A man looking for Redemption,' Halliday told him.

'You ain't anythin' to do with them?' the old man questioned as he pointed with his gun at the four men in the pens.

'Nope,' Halliday said. 'Just lookin' for Redemption, like I said. This it?'

The old man's eyes narrowed suspiciously, and then he said;

'Perdition's more like what we got here, mister. Redemption's over thataway.'

Using his gun as a pointer again, he indicated the country across the siding.

Halliday nodded.

'Far?'

'Half a day, mebbe,' the man muttered. 'Now get on your way, since you ain't got no business here with any of us.'

The man in black was leaning on the rails of the pen now, looking completely at ease. His three companions seemed less sure of themselves from the way they shuffled around and whispered among themselves.

'I'll have to get some water from the tank first,' Halliday said, and he slowly turned his horse in that direction.

He heard the old man curse, and then somebody walking behind him. When he looked over his shoulder, he saw one of the old man's cowhands stepping along in his footsteps with a six-gun in his hand.

Halliday continued on to the tank and came out of the saddle, showing no interest in what was going on behind him.

He pulled down the chute and filled the trough, filling his canteen from the gushing stream at the same time. He stood back to let the sorrel drink its fill, and then he leaned down to splash water over his face, neck and shoulders.

The cowhand was still standing a few feet behind him, just watching.

'Looks like trouble down there,' Halliday said finally.

There was no answer, and from the look of him, the haggard cowhand was just too tired to speak. He jumped and turned around when he heard the old man's voice down near the pens.

'That was warnin' shots before, Rudder,' the old

man was saying. 'Iffen you know what's good for you, you'll blame well keep your distance. Better still, get on back to McPhee and tell him he ain't tyin' up no cattle cars in this territory. I got some important business to settle with them gents you're crowdin' over there, and I ain't takin' sass from you or anybody else.'

Halliday saw a smile cross the face of the lean man in black, but the three men near him looked increasingly worried. The cowhand hitched at his gun rig and said quietly;

'It's legal, Mahoney, and I just want to show you the paper that says so. Harp McPhee booked all them boxcars months ago. You can do any kind of deal you want with these gents here, just so long as they understand that nothin' goes onto that train unless it's wearin' McPhee's brand.' He paused to let that sink in, and then he said, 'McPhee's price is five dollars a head.'

Halliday dipped his bandanna in the trough and then tied it loosely around his neck. The cowhand sent to watch him shifted back a pace and said;

'You ready now?'

Halliday shrugged and slowly inspected his horse, lifting one hoof at a time to check for stones.

'Come on, damn you!' the cowhand grated. 'You ain't so deaf you can't hear what's goin' on down there. I got to get back.'

'You can go,' Halliday told him. 'It won't bother

11

me none.'

The cowhand licked his lips as he looked toward the pens and then back at Halliday.

'No, you go ahead,' he said wearily. 'The last thing we need around here is somebody we don't know and can't trust. Just get on your hoss and ride, and everything'll be fine.'

'Everything is fine right now,' Halliday said lazily as he put his foot in the stirrup.

He meant it. The water had made all the difference. It didn't hurt, either, to know that he was only a half a day away from his destination.

He could just about see himself riding into the town after sundown in the cool of the evening. First he would see to the sorrel then have a long glass of beer, then he would follow it up with a shot of whiskey and a big, juicy steak.

The cowhand went back three steps now.

'Dammit, mister, I don't know why you have to be so ornery,' he said.

'What's so ornery about wantin' to water a tired horse?' Halliday asked mildly.

The cowhand shook his head and brought up his gun. Whatever might have come of the move was suspended by a fresh commotion down at the pens. The old man's voice was raised in anger now as he said;

'You keep the hell outta this, Rudder! I come to talk to them buyers, not some shiftless gunpacker. If McPhee has somethin' to say to me, he better say it hisself and not send no messenger boy. . . .'

'The price is five dollars a head, Mahoney,' Rudder said again. 'Take it or leave it – it's all the same to me.'

Mahoney hurled a curse across the short space between them.

'Five dollars?' the old man snorted. 'Why don't you git on back to playin' nursemaid to Harp McPhee, where you belong?'

Halliday saw the old man take a step forward, his gun held down at his side. Mahoney had taken only two steps when Rudder's hand swooped down in a move so smooth and fast it was hard to follow – a move that ended in gunfire and sent Mahoney's gun spinning out of his hand.

The cowhand ran toward the pens.

Halliday drew and fired just once. His bullet tore across the open space and shot the gun out of Rudder's hand.

'Now you two are even,' he called.

Rudder cursed and flexed his bloodied fingers, then his left hand dropped to the butt of his second gun.

'Don't try it, mister!' Halliday warned him.

Rudder's face twisted in anger as he fixed his dark eyes on Halliday.

Mahoney spun around in surprise and when he saw the smoke coiling from Halliday's gun, he asked;

'What'd you do that for, stranger?'

13

'We know each other,' Halliday said, jerking his chin at Rudder. 'You just go about your business while we catch up on the news.'

Rudder's attention was fixed completely on Halliday now. It was clear that he was trying to recall where their paths had crossed.

'The Rio Basin,' Halliday told him, 'about this time last year. I was ridin' for the Callinan outfit.'

Rudder's expression changed from anger to sneering contempt when he growled;

'Name?'

'Halliday.'

Without taking his eyes off the gunman, Halliday then addressed Mahoney;

'Well, mister, are you gonna sell some cattle or not?'

Mahoney studied him suspiciously for a moment, and then turned his attention to the three cattle buyers, who were walking back to their tethered horses.

'Where the hell do you think you're goin'?' the old man roared.

The three men dropped their shoulders and exchanged worried looks. Finally, the one with the round, red face turned to face Mahoney.

'We come out here to buy cattle,' he said. 'It ain't our fault we can't do it, so don't you go hollerin' at us. This country's dried up so bad there ain't a scrap of anything left for 'em to eat. If they can't get on

14

that train, they'll starve. What kind of fools'd buy cattle just to watch 'em starve?'

'I'll see you get boxcars,' Mahoney said grimly as he walked toward them on his stumpy legs.

The three men whispered among themselves and looked nervously at Rudder. His cold stare in response was all it took to send them on their way.

Mahoney cursed and went after them, grabbing the red-faced man by the shoulder when he caught up to them.

'I told you it's all legal, Mahoney,' Rudder drawled. 'Harp McPhee has first call on any cattle cars that go out of here. If you don't like his terms, you'll just have to drive them cattle of yours some-where else.'

Mahoney spun to face him.

'Can't do that, and you damn well know it, Rudder! There's no water between here and Toe Springs, and maybe none even at the springs by the time we'd get there. I'm not gonna stand by and watch my herd die, and I'm damned if I'm gonna be railroaded into sellin' for five dollars a head. Now keep quiet while I try to talk some sense into these poor spineless fools.'

The round-faced man had squirmed out of Mahoney's grip, and now he grabbed his horse and got it between himself and the irate rancher.

Halliday sat patiently, never taking his eyes off Rudder. He remembered him as a man who skated along the edges of the law, a man who was also good with a gun.

Rudder always had somebody to back his play back at the Rio Basin, so there was no telling how he would act on his own.

'Let's just let Mahoney talk to the buyers, Rudder,' he said. 'It's no business of ours.'

'Like hell—!' Rudder exploded.

'And none of that,' Halliday cut in. 'It's been a hard day.'

He seemed to be lounging in the saddle without a care in the world, but Mahoney's cowhands could see that he was about as relaxed as a trap set to spring.

Mahoney gave Halliday another puzzled look, but then he nodded in gratitude and turned back to face the buyer.

'Buckley, you said at my place that those cattle were as good as any you'd seen all month, considerin' the drought. So are you gonna let that feller change your mind just because he's got hisself a showy gun rig?'

Buckley wiped sweat from his red face and shifted nervously in the saddle.

'Nobody's scared, Mahoney,' he said unconvincingly. 'It's just that we got no use for cattle if we can't ship 'em out. Without them cars, we just can't do business. Can't you see that for yourself?'

'All I see is a man so scared he's shakin' in his shoes!' Mahoney snapped.

16

'Not scared,' Buckley insisted, 'sensible. I'm sure sorry, but . . . well, maybe next year.'

'Git!' Rudder said suddenly, and Buckley jumped as though he had been shot.

Halliday worked his horse a little closer to Rudder, and said, 'I told you to keep out of it, mister.'

'And I'm sayin' the same thing to you, Halliday. Mind your own damn business. The man I work for has all the boxcars in these parts booked and paid for.'

'The price he's offerin' for that man's herd just plain stinks,' Halliday said. 'This whole business stinks.'

'Then I suggest you get your nose upwind,' Rudder growled.

Halliday's mouth tightened. He looked curiously at Mahoney, and saw that the old man had run out of bluff and bluster. Now he just looked worried.

The three buyers were slowly moving away.

Mahoney's expression changed, and he swung about to confront Rudder again, and asked;

'What sense is there in keepin' this train standin' idle on the sidin'?'

'You know why,' Rudder smirked. 'Sooner or later, you'll have to sell to Mr McPhee, like it or not.'

Halliday saw Mahoney's shoulders droop. Losing most of a year's profits undoubtedly would be a terrible blow, but it almost seemed that this was something worse.

Halliday felt sorry for whatever the old man was forced to endure, but he was acutely aware that this was not his fight. He did not like Rudder, but he did not know Mahoney. Settling himself in the saddle, he began to back the sorrel away.

Mahoney looked up at him, and the sad old eyes were filled with bitter disappointment.

Halliday shrugged his heavy shoulders.

'Seems like he's holdin' all the high cards,' he muttered.

'Like hell!' Mahoney bristled. 'I'm not sellin' at his price, and that's all there is to it!'

Rudder leaned forward on the rails of the cattle pen and grinned. The buyers were still hesitant, but now they put their horses into a run.

'Five dollars was the boss' best price,' he smirked. 'Who knows? Maybe now he won't figure your cattle are worth that much.'

The gunman turned and waved toward the stationary train with its line of empty boxcars.

Almost immediately, a barrel-chested man in overalls climbed down from the engine and made his way along the rails. When he reached the gunman, he said;

'What's it to be, Mr Rudder?'

Rudder pointed to Halliday and then to Mahoney.

'If anybody tries to load them cattle cars without my say-so, what would you do?'

The man frowned and rubbed the back of his

neck. The slow grin did nothing to brighten his surly features.

'Why, I guess I'd just start shootin', Mr Rudder,' he said. 'I know who's paid for all these cars, and it ain't either one of them fellers over there.'

'If you started shootin', I guess you'd just naturally expect me to back you, wouldn't you?' Rudder asked.

'Well, naturally. It'd be you and me against whoever was tryin' to take somethin' that they didn't pay for.'

Rudder nodded and turned to Mahoney. 'You want five dollars a head now? Make up your fool mind, because I got better things to do than stand around here all day.'

Mahoney's face lost most of its color. It was plain to Halliday that the old man figured he was beaten.

He was surprised to see Mahoney square his shoulders and shake his head.

'Nope, Rudder,' the rancher said firmly. 'No deal. You suckered me into bringin' my cattle here, and you scared off my buyers . . . but, by hell, McPhee ain't goin' to make no profit outta this. So we're both gonna lose. I'll take my cattle home and get nothin' for 'em . . . and your boss is stuck payin' for a string of boxcars he can't use.'

Rudder grinned and waved the engineer back to his locomotive. Mahoney turned back to Halliday and said quietly;

'Anyways, I'm obliged for your help, mister. If I was

19

better placed, I'd invite you home for a slap-up meal and a drink or two. That'd be the least I could do . . . but the way things stand, we got some real hard drivin' ahead of us now.'

'Takin' them back home?'

'Nothin' else for me to do,' Mahoney said.

'Then I'll ride along with you, and maybe you can show me the way to Redemption.'

'Don't mind if I do,' Mahoney said, striding past Rudder as though the gunman wasn't there.

He opened the gates himself and told his men to get the cattle moving.

Halliday worked his horse across to the gate before the first of the cattle came out. He saw that they were lean but still saleable, especially if they could be freighted and fattened at the other end of the line.

Mahoney walked across to a gray mare and swung into the saddle. He was a tired old man, but he was not about to give in to a man like Harp McPhee.

Rudder waited for the cattle to clear the pens before he went to retrieve his gun and then his horse. Like his clothes and his gunrig, his gelding was black.

When he was in the saddle, the gunman looked straight at Halliday and gave an almost imperceptible nod.

'Redemption,' he said, and then he rode toward the locomotive.

Before long, the train began to puff black smoke from the stack, and then the wheels began to turn.

The cattle were moving, too, and Halliday rode ahead to chase a stray back into the tightly bunched herd.

TWO

A TOWN CALLED REDEMPTION

'Straight up the slope,' said Tom Mahoney, 'and then find your own way through the timber. The town's on the other side.'

The rancher extended his hand to Buck Halliday, and Halliday noticed the deeply etched lines of worry on the old man's face as he gripped his paw.

Halliday picked up his reins and ran them through his fingers.

'Drought might break,' he muttered.

'Might find a gold nugget in the bottom of my coffee cup, too,' Mahoney offered with weak jocularity.

The cowhands had driven the cattle to the yard

behind the ranch house and left them to forage for what little feed there was on the baked, bare ground.

Halliday gave the rancher a nod and turned the sorrel toward the slope.

He had taken coffee with Mahoney on his porch and listened to the old man's tale of woe. The rancher had come to this country ten years earlier with almost nothing to start with, but careful management and hard work had seen him amass a herd of seven hundred head, ten milkers, and a dozen quality horses.

The drought had been with them for over a year now, and any money he had saved for bad times had been eaten up by the hiring of more hands to keep his herd moving to what pasture remained.

Now that all the grass had been eaten, he had decided to sell his entire herd to meet a bank loan and settle back to wait for the good times to return. Harp McPhee had changed all that, and now Mahoney did not know what to do.

As Halliday rode over the hill and came out of the trees, he got his first look at Redemption. It looked like it had grown faster than anyone could plan it – sprawling out in all directions from the three wide streets that ran from east to west.

The sun had just set, and the air was cooler already. Lights were winking into life all over town, on the main streets and in the homes further back.

Halliday picked the liveliest of the three wide

streets and rode in slowly, taking in the storefronts, cottages, and a double-story saloon ablaze with lights and overflowing with music and the cacophony of many voices talking at once.

On the upstairs balcony, four young women gazed down into the street. Halliday grinned and returned their waves.

He turned the sorrel in toward the hitch rail and was coming out of the saddle when he heard glass breaking somewhere up the street.

When he turned to look that way, he was treated to the sight of four men, standing in the middle of the road and throwing rocks at the façade of the bank.

Another window shattered, and then the door of the bank flew open. A tall, lean man in a brocaded vest stepped out and seemed about to speak when a stone hit him squarely in the face. He staggered back inside with his hands covering his face.

Although there were plenty of people around, no one seemed to want to know about what was happening on the steps of one of the town's most substantial buildings.

Halliday went back into the saddle and set the sorrel running straight at the four men in the street. Before he could reach them, the injured man was back on the bank steps and dropping his hand to his gun butt. His hand came up and he fired wild, possibly because the blood from his head wound was affecting his vision. It was enough to make the four men turn and run, though, and they came close to ending up under the sorrel's hoofs.

As they struggled to avoid him, Halliday saw that at least two of them had their guns out.

'Get the hell away from here!' the man on the bank steps yelled, but now the four men were firing back at him.

A bullet came close to Halliday, and he ducked low in the saddle and raced the horse past the bank, dropping to the ground near the boardwalk and making a dive for the man on the steps.

They came together with a thud, and Halliday evaded a swinging fist and brought up his own hand to clamp the man's wrist and force the man back against a wall.

The four rock-throwers had disappeared now, but the man from the bank was still trying to shake Halliday free.

'Dammit, Finch, it's me – Buck Halliday.'

Finch Rogan stiffened and stared at Buck Halliday in disbelief.

A moment passed before Rogan relaxed and shrugged.

'You can let go of me now,' he muttered. 'I'm all right.'

'I hope so,' Halliday told him. 'You just about put another part in my hair when you were throwin' lead in all directions.'

Rogan wiped his bloodied face on his sleeve, and

then he glared up and down the street, which now was suddenly empty and silent.

Cursing softly, he turned and inspected the broken windows and the bullet-pitted door. Returning his gaze to Halliday, he said;

'Sorry, Buck. Hell, I figured you was one of them.'

Halliday shrugged and whistled up the sorrel. It came immediately to the hitch rail, and Halliday gave it a pat and looped the reins over the rail.

'Let's get inside and take a look at that face of yours,' Halliday said. 'Might be a good idea if you tell me what this is all about, too. . . .'

The banker grumbled something under his breath and pushed the bank door wide. Halliday followed him inside, and that was the first he saw of the young woman waiting near a table piled high with papers.

She was staring at them blankly, with the look of a rabbit too scared to run. She seemed very close to tears as she reached out for Rogan.

The banker locked the door and went to take her hand and led her deeper into the room. Their feet crunched on broken glass as they walked, and the papers on the table were covered with glass as well.

Halliday strode to the big window to look out into the street. A crowd was gathering directly across from the bank now, and it included a big man with a star on his shirtfront.

When Halliday turned back to the room, the girl had regained some of her composure. She was holding a handkerchief to a thin cut on her right cheek and looking past Rogan to Halliday.

'Thank you,' she said. 'Finch might have been killed.'

Halliday shrugged. He did not think it would have come to that. He had been more worried about Rogan killing one of the men and getting into more trouble than was warranted by some drunks throwing stones.

He had been surprised by Rogan's fierce reaction – it seemed nothing like the quiet, careful-thinking man Halliday had known years before.

Rogan went to wash his face at the basin in the back of the bank. When he returned, it was clear that there had been more blood than any serious injury, although his nose was swollen and the cut across the bridge of it would have stung.

'Well, Buck,' he said, 'I sure am glad to see you.'

'Looks like I came at the right time, huh?' Halliday said easily.

Rogan smiled, and there was a warmth in his deep-set eyes that showed he was genuine.

Halliday saw few visible changes in the man he had known except that the clothes were better – the kind of conservative attire that befitted a banker.

Rogan put his arm around the girl and said, 'Buck, this is Melissa Hahn. We're engaged to be married. You two better get to know each other.'

Halliday nodded at the girl. She was stunning, but

the only thing that seemed out of place with the demure dress and the low voice was the appraising, almost brazen stare that met Halliday's gaze.

No, not brazen, he decided. Those china-blue eyes were giving him the look of a woman who knew where she was going and what she wanted.

'What was the trouble all about, Finch?' Halliday asked.

Rogan brought up a chair for Melissa and then he fetched a bottle and three glasses from somewhere behind the teller's cage.

'I think you should have one, too,' he said as he offered the first glass to Melissa. 'It'll help settle your nerves.'

Handing the next glass to Halliday, he said;

'It's about money trouble. What else?'

'Dissatisfied customers?' Halliday asked.

'Yes. They want blood out of stones.'

Rogan patted Melissa's hand and smiled at her, but her glance went past him and settled on Halliday again.

Although he kept his attention on Rogan, Halliday could feel the woman appraising him, and he was wondering how she had recovered so quickly from the intense distress he had witnessed only minutes before.

Whatever was going on in that pretty head, there was no denying that Rogan had picked himself a woman that any man would be proud to have as his wife. Melissa Hahn was lovely, and she had the confidence that comes so naturally to a beautiful woman. And there was something more, Halliday thought for the second time, something . . . inviting. This was not one of those look – but – don't – touch looks she was giving him.

'You were so quick, Mr Halliday,' Melissa said, finally breaking the silence. 'I really thought those big oafs were going to kill Finch. . . .'

'I thought he might kill them, Melissa,' Halliday said, and he saw Rogan's mouth tighten. 'Maybe they were no-account, but to my mind, it just doesn't look right for a banker to be acting like a gunhawk.'

'A man has a right to defend himself, Buck!' Rogan snapped.

'It didn't look to me like you were in much danger until you drew that hogleg,' Halliday reasoned. 'What happened? Did you lose your temper?'

'What about this?' Rogan protested, pointing to his swollen nose.

'You never used to be that quick on the trigger, as I recall,' Halliday demurred. 'I've seen you talk your way out of a lot of scrapes that were a damn sight worse than this one. Remember that big hullabaloo in Memphis . . . what was the name of that saloon anyway?'

'That's in the past and forgotten!' Rogan snapped. 'Hell, I'd bent over backward to explain the situation to those men, but instead of listening to sense, they decided to stand outside my bank and throw rocks at me. The only thing that makes a bank work is that folks trust its manager. You let a thing like this happen tonight, and you'd have a run on the bank by first thing tomorrow.'

'Those fellers live in town then?' Halliday asked.

Before Rogan could answer, someone outside began to rattle the front door.

Halliday was closest to the street. He went first to a broken window that gave him a sideways view of the front porch. Satisfied with what he saw, he then went to the door and freed the latch.

It was the lawman Halliday had seen in the crowd across the street, and his face and neck were red with anger.

He glared at Halliday, then without so much as a glance at the young woman, he fixed his attention on Finch Rogan.

'Well,' he said, 'you sure done it this time. Somebody coulda got killed, the way you were throwin' lead so indiscriminately up and down the street.'

'I wasn't about to stand still and get stoned to death!' Rogan snapped. 'Where the hell were you anyway? And how come a mob could get so out of hand before the law took an interest, Hahn?'

'From where I stood, it looked like four men, not a mob,' the sheriff snorted.

When Halliday heard the lawman's name, he

looked back at the young woman again. He thought there was a resemblance in the shape if not the size of their slightly turned-up noses.

Rogan scowled back at the lawman.

'You oughta know that's just real trouble starts,' he said, 'when there's nobody with a mind to nip it in the bud.'

Hahn looked at the girl for the first time, and asked, 'Did you see who they were?'

'No, pa, I didn't. Someone yelled something out in the street, and then the window was smashed.'

'What about you, Rogan? Can you identify them?'

'No,' the banker said dejectedly.

'Well,' the sheriff said with a shrug, 'I guess that's it then. The way things are goin', it could've been just about anybody in town. . . .'

Rogan shot him a disgusted look but said no more. Melissa kissed him lightly on the check and said, 'It's time for me to go home now, Finch. I'm sure there'll be no more trouble.' Turning to her father, she said, 'Are you coming, pa?'

When Hahn shook his head, she said;

'Well, I'll see you tomorrow then.' She looked back at Halliday from the doorway and said, 'Good night. I expect I'll see more of you.'

When they could no longer hear her light footsteps on the boardwalk, Halliday pulled a tobacco pouch from his pocket and began to make himself a cigarette, all the while knowing that Hahn was still watching him. Then the lawman asked;

'What about you?'

'What about me, Sheriff?'

'Got a name you ain't scared to tell, mister?'

Halliday studied the lawman over the flame of his vesta.

'Buck Halliday.'

'You got a reason for showin' your face around these parts?'

Halliday drew on the cigarette and took his time to answer, letting the smoke trail from his nostrils.

'Finch is an old pard of mine, and I always said I'd look him up one day. Today is the day.'

Hahn gave Halliday and Rogan an icy glare as he moved to the door.

'On your way,' he said to the small crowd that still lingered outside the bank's door. 'Trouble's over and it doesn't have a thing to do with you, anyway.'

The sheriff went on his way without looking back, closing the heavy door behind him.

'Well, Finch?' Halliday asked.

'Well what?' Rogan snapped.

'I think it's time you explained what's goin' on here, don't you? There's more to this than meets the eye. Like I said, you're not actin' the way I remember. Once you would've told those fellers where to go and let it go at that. What's brought about the change in you?'

Rogan sighed and dropped into the chair beside

the table. There was a minute's silence and then his hand shot out and swept the papers and broken glass to the floor.

'It's been awhile, Buck.'

'Four years.'

'Yeah. If I had the chance to do it all over again, I think I would've stuck with what I had. There's worse things than eating dust all day.'

'What's so bad about this that you can't handle it, Finch?' Halliday asked.

'Never said I couldn't handle it.'

'You didn't need to,' Halliday told him, drawing on the cigarette and putting one foot up against the table. 'What is it that folks in this town have against you?'

'The problem is that they're all fools!' Rogan barked. 'They all want what I haven't got.'

'Money?'

'Money! They want bucket-loads of it, and I can't help them anymore. I've done all I can.'

Halliday pursed his lips thoughtfully.

'The bank's run out of money?'

'Cleaned out. Worse still, it's in debt. I've dredged up every cent I could find – my own money and everything my father left me. You'd think that would satisfy them, wouldn't you? But no. They want more.'

Halliday pinched his cigarette out and tossed the butt into the waste basket.

'They know all that, Finch?'

'Sure, they know. I've told them often enough. I've even opened the books for them to examine. Anybody who wanted to look at the ledgers was welcome to do it. All the bank holds is some useless mortgages on properties of no value. If the drought doesn't break soon, this whole town will be finished. I've slaved for four years trying to make a go of this bank. I can tell you, it was no fun being penned up in here day after day, trying my damnedest to do everything right. I was mighty careful not to take on any bad risks, and I protected people from borrowing more than they could afford to pay back. I listened to their stories and kept their secrets and did everything I could for this town, and now they turn around and want to spit in my face. I've had a bellyful, Buck. I'm sick to the teeth of the whole lot of them!'

'Have you tried to get some backers from the big cities back East?' Halliday asked him. 'There must be money men back there who can see the possibilities. Droughts do break, you know.'

Rogan got to his feet so fast that he banged his hip on the side of the table. Rubbing his side and cursing to himself, he said, 'I've tried everywhere. I had a source of funds right here in town, but it dried up on me. . . .'

'Let's have a drink and think about it,' Halliday suggested. 'Maybe we can come up with a name or two. There's always someone who can benefit from hard times such as these, and that's who you want.'

'Not in this town,' Rogan muttered. 'I've got every dollar of investment I could wheedle out of folks, and I've handed it on. I've taken up mortgages for a client who is left with nothing himself if things don't improve. This whole part of the country is flat busted, Buck. The people here know it, and they're blaming me for everything from dry wells to their sick kids. They took a risk listening to my advice, and it didn't pay off for them.'

It still seemed to Halliday that Rogan was holding something back from him, but he made no further comment.

They went out onto the boardwalk together, but when Halliday headed down to the street, Rogan said;

'I'll catch up with you later, Buck. Maybe one more try won't hurt.'

'Suit yourself, Finch,' Halliday said, and watched Rogan go off alone.

Halliday had just reached the hitch rail when he heard a gun bark. He looked up in time to see the shape of a man, bent over and running across the roof.

The bullet had come within an inch of his head, and nowhere near Rogan's.

His hand flashed down and then he drew a careful bead. It was a long shot, but he was satisfied to see that he had clipped the man.

Now he heard a startled cry from Rogan further down the boardwalk. With the six-gun still in his hand, Halliday sprinted in the banker's direction.

At first, he could see nothing on the street. He stopped at the mouth of the first alley and heard running footsteps. He decided to keep to the main street, and he finally caught sight of movement overhead.

Starlight gleamed on the barrel of a gun and then came the red flare of the gunshot.

Halliday dived sideways and came up shooting at the sniper who was almost directly above his head. He heard the grunt and then the desperate scrambling as the man struggled to keep his footing but eventually lost his balance. The man's body bent forward, head lowered, and hung for a moment from the eaves before he fell, an empty boot still dangling from the edge of the roof.

Dead or alive, the man was showing no signs that he was conscious. Halliday turned him over onto his back, but it was too dark to see the face, and now someone was running in his direction.

Sheriff Hahn and Finch Rogan arrived almost at the same time, as a curious crowd began to gather.

THREE

HARP MCPHEE

'Halliday!'

Sheriff Luther Hahn spat the name like a curse as he came to a halt with his big hands on his hips. Halliday pointed to the dead man and said;

'He fired at me from the roof. I managed to wing him but he kept after me. That didn't leave me much choice, Sheriff.'

'Just like that, huh?' Hahn growled, scowling blackly at him. 'You're just strollin' down the street, mindin' your own damn business, and a stranger climbs up on the roof to take a potshot at you?'

'Just like that, Sheriff,' Halliday said, 'unless you can tell me who the feller was and come up with a better explanation—'

'That's how it looked to me,' Rogan cut in quickly.

'We left the bank soon after you did, Luther, and we each went off in our own direction. Then I heard the first shot and saw the man running across the roof of the store.' He pointed to the building and added, 'Buck shot back at him. I thought he missed, but he started down the street toward me and I couldn't see the sniper on the roof anymore. When Buck fired again, I saw this feller fall.' He looked down at the man at their feet and added, 'I don't see how you can possibly blame—'

'Nobody's askin' you to see anythin'!' Hahn growled.

Rogan wanted to take it further, but Halliday looked at him slyly and shook his head. Touching the man on the ground with the toe of his boot, Halliday said;

'Seems to me it's about time to give some thought to what's goin' on around here. This was no drunken cowboy havin' some harmless fun, and it sure wasn't a stray bullet that almost split my skull open like a watermelon.'

Hahn's face showed his reluctance to follow the advice, but after a moment's struggle with his temper, he called for a light. Someone brought a lantern, and Hahn held it down close to the dead man's upturned face.

The sheriff frowned. Rogan looked puzzled.

Although Halliday was the most surprised of all, he kept that to himself. The dead man was the engineer from Harp McPhee's cattle train – the train that would not carry cattle unless it was at McPhee's say-so.

'You know him, Sheriff?' Halliday asked.

Hahn shook his head and said, 'Nope, I sure as hell don't. How about you?'

Halliday shook his head and shrugged.

'You real sure about that?' Hahn persisted. 'Maybe you recollect just some little thing like where you locked horns with him last time. . . .'

Halliday shook his head again.

A short silence followed, with the whole street so quiet that Halliday could hear the lawman's heavy breathing through his nose, like a bull preparing for a charge.

'Then why the hell would he want to take a shot at you?' Hahn exploded.

'Maybe he mistook me for somebody else,' Halliday suggested.

He was asking himself the same question the sheriff had posed when a little man pushed past Hahn and bent over the dead man.

'Why, damn you?' the little man said thickly with his eyes turned up to Halliday. 'Why'd you kill him?'

'Self-defense,' Halliday told the man flatly.

The little man straightened and lunged at him, but Halliday coolly caught him by the shoulder and spun him around toward the sheriff.

'Self-defense, like hell!' the little man shouted. 'Jake here was never one for gunplay. You killed him, so it's murder!'

Halliday looked over the little man's head at Hahn.

'Seems you've got somebody who knew this feller, Sheriff,' he said.

The crowd had doubled in size and was pressing in close to hear what was said.

Hahn noticed the growing crowd, too, and without releasing the grip he had taken on the little man's shoulder, he swung around and bellowed, 'Get away from here, all of you! Give us some damn room!'

The crowd moved back but did not disperse. Hahn glowered at Halliday and said;

'And you keep quiet, mister. I'm the one that's gonna do the talkin' to this feller!'

'I wish you'd get on with it then, Sheriff,' Halliday said innocently.

The sheriff turned his cold stare on the little man, who was squirming in his grip now.

'Who the hell are you?' Hahn snarled.

'Name's Will Cross.'

'And him?' Hahn asked, pointing to the dead man.

'Jake Sharp,' Cross said.

Hahn nodded as if at last he was getting some-where.

'OK, now what about Halliday? You ever see him before?'

Cross looked bleakly at Halliday, and swore.

'Nope, I ain't seen him before, but by hell, I'll see him later! Ain't nobody gonna shoot down a friend of mine in—'

'Enough!' Hahn rasped. 'Did Jake Sharp ever mention Halliday to you?'

The little man shook his head.

'Then why do you suppose this pard of yours was up on a roof in the middle of the night tryin' to shoot Halliday's lights out?' Hahn asked. 'I can smell the whiskey on your breath – does that mean the two of you were drinkin' together, and Sharp mistook Halliday for somebody else. Is that what happened?'

'Don't know,' Cross said. 'Jake only had one drink, and then he told me he had somebody to see, was all. Next thing I heard was the gunshots, same as everybody else.'

Cross pulled himself away from the sheriff, glaring up at Halliday as he strode away.

Hahn wiped sweat from his brow and confronted Halliday again.

'OK, mister, seems you're in the clear – this time,' he growled. 'But the fact remains that you're the one that drew this trouble here, one way or the other. You just got into town tonight, and you've already got yourself into two gunfights. I want you gone before mornin', or I'll lock you up for disturbin' the peace.'

'To tell you the truth,' Halliday grinned, 'your town isn't the kind of place I'd choose to stay any longer than I have to, Sheriff.'

As he sauntered off with Rogan beside him, Halliday said;

'I think we've earned a drink, and besides, I think it's a good idea for us to talk to you some more. How about you line us up a nice big glass of beer while I see to my horse?'

Rogan gave him directions to the livery stables, and Halliday went back to the bank where the sorrel was still tied to the hitching rail.

When the horse was stabled, Halliday took a short-cut through the alley that came out beside the saloon. As he walked beside the vacant lot behind the saloon, he saw a tiny red glow near the saloon's back door.

Maybe somebody had stepped out for some fresh air . . . or for some peace and quiet . . . or to take another shot at him. . . ?

With a sigh, Halliday slid his six-gun up and down in its holster and then he cut across the yard until he was only a few feet from the man with the cigarette.

'Howdy, Rudder,' he said.

'I hear you been cuttin' up rough in this town,' Rudder smirked.

'It's been a busy night, true enough – too bad about that friend of yours.'

'Ain't you had enough for one night without pushin' me?' Rudder said tightly.

'I didn't go lookin' for any of it, mister,' Halliday

replied flatly.

He was surprised to see Rudder hold back. It seemed that for some reason, the gunman did not want more trouble tonight.

Halliday knew that Rudder was not afraid of him, and he knew for a fact that the man had no aversion to spilling blood. Once he had seen him cut down three men in a saloon and chase the fourth outside to fill him with lead while the fellow was running for his life.

Whatever Rudder was up to now, it suited Halliday to give him some breathing space.

'Sharp worked for the railroad, not for me,' Rudder said as Halliday stepped past him to get to the back door of the saloon. 'I take care of my own business.'

'That's what I figured,' Halliday muttered.

'You figured right then.'

Halliday found Finch Rogan surrounded by angry men who all seemed to be talking at once.

With his back against the bar and his hand wrapped around an empty glass, Rogan was listening in tight-lipped silence.

Halliday moved straight to the back of the crowd and said quietly, 'Excuse me, gentlemen.'

He forced his way between the shoulders of two of the men and elbowed them aside. Then he pushed forward, making the tightly-packed bunch give him room.

43

He took money from his pocket and placed it on the counter near Rogan's elbow and took Rogan's glass from his hand.

'Refill, Finch?'

The crowd had gone quiet and now there was a cleared circle around Halliday and Rogan as the two men tasted their drinks and talked quietly between themselves. Finally, someone behind Halliday asked, 'What's your game, mister? We seen you ride in, we seen you outside the bank, and we seen you where that feller got shot dead. Are you tryin' to see how many enemies you can make in one night or what?'

Halliday glanced casually over his shoulder to look at the red-faced individual he had been watching all the time in the bar mirror.

'I came to Redemption to look up an old friend,' he said casually. 'Now I've found him, and all I want is to chew the fat with him and maybe get a little drunk. Does that bother you in some way?'

'Yeah, it does,' the man snapped. 'My name's Jeff Leonard. I run the Mercantile.'

'If I need anything, I'll come see you,' Halliday said quietly.

'Don't you sass me, mister!' Leonard said loudly. 'I can see you're here to side with Rogan, but you don't scare me one bit. Rogan sold us out, and that's all there is to it.'

'By lendin' you money when you asked for it?' Halliday asked.

Leonard snorted and two of the other towners began to speak, but the big man silenced them with an impatient gesture.

'No, let me handle this,' he snapped as he pointed a thick finger at Finch Rogan. 'He loaned us money, all right, and he also tied us down so tight that we had to sign over everythin' we owned to get it. Now all we got is debts and a whole lot of bloodsuckers gettin' ready to foreclose on everythin' we've worked for.'

Halliday looked at Rogan to see if he had anything to say, but Rogan kept his back turned and his hand on his glass.

'Leonard,' Halliday said, 'you tell me you're a businessman, ain't that right?'

'I am,' the big man confirmed for him with a trace of pride.

'So I guess you know enough never to sign anythin' without readin' it first. . . .'

Leonard scowled blackly.

'Well?' Halliday prodded.

'Yeah, I read it,' Leonard muttered.

'So you know what would happen if you couldn't come up with the repayments. Right?'

Leonard's face went white and he nodded grimly.

'What that says to me,' Halliday continued, 'is that you were in deep trouble a long time before today, and you came runnin' to Rogan askin' for his help. He got you the money you said you needed. You're

45

the ones that went back on the deal, not Rogan. You signed a paper, promisin' to pay back what you owed . . . but you didn't keep your promise, did you?'

Leonard flashed a sullen look Rogan's way.

'He loaned us money and said there'd be more. He said all we had to do was stick together – for us to back the cattlemen and farmers and for him to back us. OK, so we gave credit to anybody who wanted it, and borrowed money to stock up again, and now that stock's about gone. And we ain't been paid, so we can't meet the damned loan. They're gonna close this whole town down. . . .'

'They?' Halliday asked quietly.

Leonard pointed at Rogan again, and said;

'The bank! Who else do you think? He's the one that's got our mortgages.'

'I'm only holding them, Leonard!' Rogan snapped in his first show of defiance. 'The bank's cleaned out. I had to act in the interests of a customer.'

'And who might that be?' Leonard sneered. 'Just give us his name. Maybe we'll go see him.'

Rogan shook his head.

'I'm afraid I can't divulge the man's name, Leonard. I told you that before. I have an agreement with him that holds me down to—'

'Then you're lyin',' Leonard jeered. 'There ain't nobody in this but you. You tricked us with all your big talk and fancy promises. You're nothin' but a goddamn thief, and I'm sayin' it loud and clear.'

Rogan lunged forward and socked Leonard on the jaw. The big man rocked back on his heels, more shocked than hurt as he stumbled into three of his companions.

'You damn well asked for that, Leonard,' Rogan muttered. 'My hands are tied, and you'll just have to think what you like – think it, but don't say it. I've had about all I can take of your ranting and raving, and your endless complaints. Leave me be!'

Leonard rubbed his jaw. The other towners seemed to be watching his lead.

'OK then, Rogan,' Leonard said. 'I guess it'll all come out in the open soon enough. But there's one thing you oughtta know. I don't intend to sit still and get cheated out of everything I've worked for. I'll fight you down to the last floorboard before I give up my store. I'd do it alone if I had to, but the difference between you and me is I've got friends in the same sticky mess. We're gonna fight this all the way. We've got no damn choice.'

Leonard wiped sweat from his face, turned on his heel and strode noisily across the room. The others quickly followed.

Halliday blew out a loud breath and said, 'He sure does have a bee in his bonnet, Finch. Best watch him.'

Instead of answering, Rogan threw his drink down in one gulp and busied himself with refilling the glass from the bottle on the counter.

Halliday watched this performance in silence, and then he said;

'What's this feller's name you keep talkin' about, Finch?'

Rogan shook his head.

'Would it be Harp McPhee?'

Rogan dropped his gaze and failed to respond.

'Figured as much. Seems you've been swallowed up by a bigger fish.'

Rogan swung to angrily confront him.

'What the hell are you talking about, Buck? What the blazes do you know about this, anyway?'

Halliday told him what he had seen on the railroad siding on his way into town. When he described how Tom Mahoney had refused McPhee's five dollars a head and taken his herd home to die, Rogan thumped his fist despairingly on the counter.

'Dammitall,' he said hoarsely, 'you're right. I was a gullible little fish and that bastard has swallowed me up, and everybody else in the county with me! The money he put into the bank was the bait that did it. Everybody borrowed, and now McPhee owns the lot.'

'And I guess it's all legal?' Halliday asked softly.

Rogan went to move away, but Halliday put his hand out to restrain him.

'Sit still and think it out, Finch,' he advised.

Rogan shook his hand away, saying, 'I can't. I've got to do something!'

'Like what?'

'Like finding McPhee and wringing his goddamn neck for him.'

'That's just what he'd be expectin' you to do,' Halliday said. 'You don't have to give him everything he wants. He's got enough already. I'll hang around and you just go about your business, same as usual, and wait for McPhee to make his play. Leonard's gonna fight him, and so is Tom Mahoney. There'll be others who'll back them.'

'Lord knows what good it'll do them,' Rogan said sourly.

From the corner of his eye, Halliday saw Rudder return to the saloon, smiling faintly to himself.

Halliday understood now that the gunman was the walking, talking proof of McPhee's business acumen. The wheeler-dealer had planned everything to the last detail, right down to hiring Rudder for the time when people began to suspect just who was behind all their troubles.

'Somethin' will turn up, Finch,' Halliday said quietly. 'In the meantime, why don't you get outta here and go see that pretty girl of yours? From what I saw of her, she has what it takes to make a man forget his troubles.'

'She's a fine woman, Buck,' Rogan said stiffly.

'Nobody said otherwise, Finch,' Halliday said calmly. 'That's why you'll be better off spending a few hours with her instead of tryin' to drown your troubles here. Who knows? Somethin' might turn up in the morning. Worries always seem easier to handle in the daylight, I've noticed.'

Rogan finished his drink and suddenly lifted his head, a hopeful gleam appearing in his eyes.

'Yeah,' he said, slapping his palm down on the counter. 'Melissa! Why didn't I think of it before?'

'She got money?' Halliday asked.

It seemed unlikely that a lawman's daughter would have the kind of money to measure up to Harp McPhee.

'I made some investments for her, and they paid off well,' Rogan said. 'Hell, I made plenty for her in the beginning, and she's no spendthrift. There might be enough to help Tom Mahoney, anyway. That will be a start. Then we can look for ways to prop up the others, maybe even Jeff Leonard.'

Rogan grinned and extended his hand.

'I knew you'd be a help to me, Buck, but I never figured you'd be givin' me financial advice. Thanks, pard.'

Rogan was heading briskly for the door when the batwings swung inward and a tall, prosperous-looking man stepped into the room. He stood there for a moment, surveying the saloon as though he owned it.

Halliday knew without asking that this could only be Harp McPhee. He turned his back to the bar and leaned on his elbows, content to wait to see what would develop.

The batwings swung in again and old Tom Mahoney marched in with his worn-down boot heels thumping the floor at every step.

'McPhee!' Mahoney grated. 'Did you really think I'd go for that deal of yours? I'd run the whole damn herd off a cliff before I'd see you profit from the hard times that's hit this county!'

'Business is business,' McPhee said over his shoulder.

Mahoney followed him into the saloon, but suddenly Rudder was there, grabbing the tough old man by the shoulder and pulling him away.

'Mr McPhee don't like to be bothered,' the gunman said. 'You better get a hold of yourself, mister.'

Mahoney rocked back on his heels, his face going scarlet with rage. It was clear that he was intending to go for Rudder, but Finch Rogan got to him first and restrained him.

'Hold on, Tom,' the banker said quickly. 'Tell me just how much is owin' on your place and what the due date is. . . .'

Mahoney glared at him resentfully.

'You oughta know that, Rogan! You was the one that sucked me into the deal and—'

'Tom!' Rogan snapped. 'You're not the only man around here that's in debt, you know. I don't carry around all those facts and figures in my head. Just stop snapping and snarling for a minute and tell me what I'm asking.'

McPhee had moved away from the two and was standing beside Rudder now. His stare was fixed on Rogan, and his expression had changed from smug satisfaction to annoyance.

The usual saloon uproar of clinking glasses and competing conversations had died away to an enthralled silence.

Cowhands, cattlemen, farmers and townsmen all strained to hear the old rancher's answer.

'A thousand damn dollars, and it's due on the day after tomorrow.'

Rogan smiled at him.

'Then you can quit worrying, Tom,' he said. 'You'll get your money, at normal rates of interest with any extensions you need, too. Come to the bank first thing in the morning.'

Mahoney's jaw dropped.

'I hope you ain't kiddin' me,' he said slowly.

'When did you ever know a banker to make jokes about money?' Rogan said with a grin. 'I've got things to do now, so I'll leave you to it. Come and see me in the morning.'

Mahoney seemed to be rooted to the spot. He had the look of a man who wanted to have hope but could not quite bring himself to risk it. Then he spotted Buck Halliday, and Halliday jerked his chin as an invitation to join him.

McPhee and his gunman had stepped away from the crowd now and seemed to be deep in serious conversation. Finally, McPhee nodded and went back to the door without ever taking a drink. Rudder ambled over to a card game and watched without much interest as the gamblers played a couple of hands. At least to Halliday, it was clear that the gunman had other things on his mind.

'Hey, Tom,' Halliday said. 'You look like a man who could use a drink. . . .'

FOUR

A WOMAN MAKES HER MOVE

Tom Mahoney was finishing his drink and grinning at Buck Halliday when gunfire cut through the late-night quiet of the street, sending the saloon crowd into shocked silence.

Halliday turned casually to scan the bunch in the saloon.

Rudder was still there, and he gave Halliday a mocking grin when their eyes met and locked.

'Got to see about this, Tom,' Halliday said, and went for the street at a run.

He was just in time to see Finch Rogan staggering toward the bank. The banker almost made it to the steps, but then his legs buckled and he was falling to the ground.

Halliday was the first to reach him, only a few seconds before Sheriff Luther Hahn came running.

'Where are you hit?' Halliday asked, but then he saw the answer for himself.

Blood was already soaking through Rogan's jacket, just below the shoulder.

'Dammit!' Rogan whispered. 'It ain't the first time, but I still purely hate getting shot.'

'Know what you mean,' Halliday agreed, and then the sheriff was puffing and blowing beside them.

'Not you again, Halliday?' Hahn snarled.

'Don't you think it's more important to get this man out of the street?' Halliday snapped back at him. 'Come on, give me a hand.'

Silently, the two men helped Rogan to his feet.

All the while, Halliday's eyes were sweeping the street, first at ground level and then along the rooftops.

The only sign of life came from the saloon as the patrons crowded cautiously out onto the boardwalk.

Rogan was swaying on his feet now, but when the sheriff reached out to steady him, the banker pushed him away.

'All right then,' Hahn said, 'tell me who did it.'

'How the hell would I know?' Rogan said weakly. 'In case you haven't noticed, it's dark out here!'

'Don't snap at me!' Hahn said with rising anger. 'It ain't my fault you stopped a bullet. And I only asked you a simple question.'

'Well, I don't have a simple answer,' Rogan snarled, 'but there's one thing I can tell you. It wasn't anybody that owes money to the bank, so don't waste your time thinking it was. Try looking somewhere close to Harp McPhee.'

'Judas!' Hahn breathed. 'Do you know what you're sayin'?'

'You asked me, and I'm tellin' you,' Rogan whispered.

'Well, you better think twice about—'

'Leave him be, Sheriff,' Halliday said. 'The man's been shot, after all.'

'That don't give him the right to accuse somebody when he doesn't have the proof. Why—'

Rogan began to go limp in Halliday's grip, but Halliday held him upright.

Ignoring the lawman as though he were no longer there, Halliday said;

'You're gonna have to tell me where to find the doctor, Finch.'

They left the sheriff standing there as they moved haltingly along the boardwalk with Halliday following Rogan's directions.

When Rogan was lying on the table in the doctor's office, Halliday touched his arm and said;

'Now you just take it easy and don't move. This is as good a place as any to spend the night.'

Rogan opened his eyes and winced as the doctor

cut away the bloodied coat and shirt to inspect the wound.

When the medic stepped away from the table, Halliday went with him, and the doctor muttered;

'Likely chipped a bone, but the bullet went straight through. He won't be laid up for long, but it's going to take time to get that arm working right again.'

'Can you keep him here for the night?' Halliday asked.

'I could, but I don't see that it's necessary.'

'Buck?' Rogan was calling from the table. 'Go tell Melissa I'm all right but that I have to see her tonight. Tell her I'll come as soon as I can. . . .'

'Just let the doctor do his job,' Halliday said as he stepped outside.

Hahn was waiting for him, leaning against the wall with his arms folded.

'So?' the lawman asked when he straightened.

'He'll live, Sheriff. So where can I find your daughter this time of night?'

'I can't see why she has to be disturbed in the middle of the night over this,' Hahn argued.

'Just tell me where she is.'

Hahn gave Halliday a stern look, but he said;

'You just steer clear of my girl. There's been nothin' but trouble ever since you set foot in this town, and I sure don't want you dumpin' it on her doorstep. I never liked the idea of Rogan hangin' around her, and I figure Melissa is now beginnin' to wake up to herself. Stay away from her, Halliday, and don't forget that I want you outta town by mornin'.'

Halliday let out a long, gusty sigh. He could see that with Rogan laid up and Rudder riding high, there was nothing to be gained by ruffling the sheriff's feathers anymore than necessary.

'I don't expect there'll be trouble from now on,' he said reasonably. 'It could be that you'll finish up with a real nice town again before long.'

He could feel the sheriff's angry stare burning holes in his back as he walked away, but his mind was on other things, all of them to do with the shady Harp McPhee. They included McPhee's interference in the sale of Mahoney's cattle, McPhee putting the squeeze on Rogan's bank, McPhee putting a gunman like Rudder on his payroll. . . .

They all added up to an unpleasant smell hanging heavy over what apparently had been a quiet town with a bright future.

Like a chess player deciding on his next move, Halliday was turning over the possible ways that he might be able to help Finch Rogan. The banker had been as good a friend as a man could ever hope to have, and now he was downhearted.

He passed the saloon on the opposite side of the street and headed for the edge of town. The street was briefly busy again with cowhands galloping back to their distant ranches and bunkhouses, and

towners wondering how to slip in the door without
waking their wives. By the time Halliday reached the
spot where the street played out in a network of ruts
and dried-out potholes, Redemption was settling
down for a last few hours of sleep before the coming
of a new day.

He smoked one last cigarette and started back,
thinking mainly of how it would feel to lie down in a
real bed for a change.

He was stepping back onto the boardwalk when he
saw Melissa Hahn emerge from an office not more
than twenty yards ahead of him.

Halliday slipped into the shadow thrown by an
awning and stood still. He saw the woman turn back
to the doorway and lean forward on tiptoe. A black-
coated arm caught her by the waist, and it appeared
that she was lifting her face to be kissed. Then a deep
voice drifted out of the building, saying;

'Hell, can't you two wait? Well, girl, go and do what
you have to.'

From the way she straightened, it appeared that
Melissa was annoyed by the remark, but she stepped
out of the embrace and for the first time, Halliday
saw that Melissa had been in the arms of Wes Rudder,
McPhee's hired gun.

'He's right,' Rudder was saying. 'Just a couple
more days, and then we can please ourselves. . . .'

Melissa seemed to accept what was said, and she
started off at once with the quick, no-nonsense walk

of a woman out late and on her own.

Halliday trailed along behind her until he saw her turn in at a big, plain building with the paint peeling on the wide-boarded siding. The simple sign mounted on a fence post in the front yard told all there was to know;

ROOMS

He stepped quietly on to the front porch and watched through the half-glass door. It appeared that she had asked the night clerk for writing implements. The man yawned and handed her a slip of paper and a pen. Melissa jotted something down on the paper, folded it neatly and returned it to the man with a smile.

Halliday waited until she had gone upstairs before he opened the door and stepped inside.

'Help you, stranger?' the night clerk asked.

'A room for the night,' Halliday told him.

'Two dollars, payable in advance. You like to sign the book?'

'Might as well,' Halliday told him, and the man turned the register around and held out the pen.

It was still warm from Melissa's hand.

Halliday scribbled his name and laid the pen and two silver dollars on the counter. The clerk handed him a key and Halliday was halfway to the stairs when the night man called him back.

'Wait a minute, mister,' he said. 'I just saw your name in the book. You're Halliday, right?'

'Right.'

'Well, I'll be doggoned,' he was saying as he fished Melissa's note out of his vest pocket. 'You only just missed each other. Miss Melissa left this message for you.'

Halliday's eyebrows rose as he read the note.

'Not bad news, I hope?' the night clerk said with hearty exuberance.

'Depends on how you look at it,' Halliday said vaguely as he headed for the stairs again.

Melissa's note said she was in Room 7 and would like to see him if he came in. His own was Room 11, at the far end of the corridor. Halliday passed her room and saw lamplight shining under her door.

He went past and let himself into his room, softly closing the door behind him. When he had lit the lamp, he sat on the bed and read Melissa's note again.

Melissa Hahn . . . the sheriff's daughter and Finch Rogan's fiancée, but apparently tied in with McPhee somehow and mighty friendly with Harp McPhee's hired gun.

Halliday decided that for the first time since he hit town, luck might be starting to turn his way. If he had not been in just the right place at the right time, he would not have seen the woman with Rudder. It appeared that Melissa did not know she had been seen on the street. It also seemed that she was not overly concerned about her injured fiancé or her

61

lawdog father.

He washed his torso in the china basin on the washstand and dried his face on a towel that had seen better days. Then he built himself a cigarette and smoked it down.

'OK, Miss Melissa,' he said softly to himself, 'let's find out what you're up to. . . .'

When he was in the hallway, he locked the door and left the key on the dusty sill.

Melissa opened the door almost as soon as he reached it, studying him curiously and smiling. Then she stepped back and said;

'Come in, Mr Halliday.'

She slid the bolt across the door as he stepped past her. Halliday noticed that her hair was freshly brushed and it seemed that she had just applied some perfume that smelled of fresh flowers.

He crossed to the window and looked down on a town that now seemed so peaceful that it was hard to believe any trouble could ever disturb it.

'I'm glad you could come, Mr Halliday,' she said. 'I'm just so terribly worried.'

'Worried?' Halliday asked, turning to look at her.

She lifted one hand and flicked back her hair. It settled around her shoulders like fine silk. Then she gave him another smile, and the warmth of it showed in her eyes.

'It's Finch,' she explained. 'He never said very much about you, only mentioned you once or twice.

Naturally, I had no reason to take any interest in you myself . . . but now you are here, I must admit that has changed.'

'So,' Halliday said gravely, 'what is it that has a nice lady like you so worried?'

'How close are you and Finch?' Melissa asked.

'Close enough. We rode together.'

'But you never entered into any business arrangements together, did you?'

Halliday pursed his lips.

'Bought a few head of cattle a couple times. Fattened them and sold them for a tidy profit.'

'He should still be doing something like that,' Melissa said quietly. 'He does not belong in a bank. He doesn't fit into town life, either. He's tried, I know, and for a time I believed he could do it. But now I know he's got himself into something he simply can't handle. He's got the whole town hating him . . . and I can't stand it.'

Halliday let his eyebrows rise into a quizzical arch.

'I figured that when a woman took up with a man she went along with everything he did – the good and the bad.'

Melissa flicked her hair back again and came across to him. Her eyes were bright and she moistened her lips with the tip of her tongue before she spoke again.

'If a woman did take up with a man, she would do that, Buck. But I've never ever told Finch that I loved him. True, I may have led him to believe there was a chance for us, but it never came to anything definite.'

'No engagement?' Halliday asked.

Melissa shook her head, and the light caught the silky hair and made Halliday want to reach out and touch it.

He could see the open invitation in her eyes, but it was even more obvious in the way she moved.

It just didn't figure, but if it was a trap, what did she hope to achieve? Halliday told himself to stay wary and let her play the game out. From the gleam in her eyes, it looked like being one hell of a game . . . and the most enjoyable in town.

'I have never been in love with Finch,' the girl said firmly, and her gaze settled searchingly on Halliday, probing for his reaction. 'And now I know I never will be. I'll be leaving soon. For some strange reason, I wanted you to know that.'

'Why will you be leaving?' Halliday asked her bluntly.

Melissa touched her lips with the wet, pink tip of her tongue again. Then her hand strayed to the top button of her shirtwaist, toying with it momentarily before beginning to undo the dainty pearl buttons one by one.

Halliday's eyes dropped to the swell of her breasts, and she said finally;

'Because Finch has disappointed me. He's let this

town down, Buck, and he's let me down, too. I've tried so hard to move him, but he's a cold man by nature. Did you know that, Buck? I'm not ashamed to admit that I have feelings – strong feelings. I need a real man, Buck. I've seen how you handle yourself, and I couldn't help but compare you with Finch. . . .'

She was standing very close to him now, undoing the last button.

Halliday felt his pulse begin to race.

'There's some kind of devil in you, Melissa,' he said slowly.

'Maybe there is,' Melissa laughed, 'but I can be nice to you. Very, very nice. Will you tell me one thing, Buck Halliday – are you going to stay in Redemption?'

'I'm not one for stayin' anywhere for long,' he told her honestly.

'Then why don't you come with me? Finch is ruined, and the town along with him. People are starting to walk off their farms. Before long, the stores will have to close. Only a fool would stay here now. We could go to Cheyenne. . . .'

When she lifted her arms and linked them loosely around his neck, Halliday told himself;

'She's not Finch's woman, and if Rudder thinks he has his brand on her, that's his problem.'

'I want you, Buck Halliday,' she whispered, pressing herself hard up against him. 'And I mean to have you.'

Halliday put one finger under her chin and tilted her head back until he could stare straight into her eyes.

'What about Finch?'

'I told you all there is to know about Finch and me. He wants me, it's true, but all he's done is shame me. He was very quick to tell everybody that I was his woman, so now the whole town acts as though we were in cahoots, frittering away their money. He can't be a friend of yours, either. . . .'

'What's that supposed to mean?' Halliday asked with a frown.

'You haven't bothered to see each other for four years.'

'I've had my own life to lead,' he told her, and then his hand went to the small of her back, holding her against his chest.

Melissa was undoing the buttons of his shirt now, and then her hands were stroking the hard, muscled chest.

'I can't help but wonder what this is all about,' Halliday muttered, but he knew that the answer had ceased to matter to both of them.

Maybe Melissa was bait for some kind of trap. Maybe every word she spoke was a lie. But for now at least, her body was doing the talking and he was keen to listen.

She turned her face up to his, and her lips opened in soft invitation.

He held her there with her body arching so that her mouth was on his mouth and her thighs were pressed hard against his groin, enjoying the prospect of the pleasure that was to come.

'Buck?'

She whispered his name so softly it was no more than a sigh.

'Yeah?'

'Let me go.'

He released her and she backed across the room to the bed, never taking her eyes from him.

She shrugged out of the blouse and let it fall from her shoulders. Then she reached back with one hand and twitched at her skirt until it fell around her ankles. Then she sat on the edge of the bed and extended one dainty foot out to him.

Obligingly, he bent down and removed the button shoes, noticing for the first time that they were red. She was already plucking at the lacy bodice, but he said;

'Let me do that.'

She nodded knowingly and lay back on the bed with her hair fanned out across the pillow and her hands at her sides, her eyes warm with invitation.

She lay there passively as he undressed her, but he saw that she was quivering with expectation wherever the soft silk or his rough hand brushed her skin.

Finally, she was naked and radiant in the lamp-light, but she remained motionless. Only her eyes moved, following his every move.

Halliday leaned over her and began to caress her throat and then her breasts. As soon as his cradled her soft bosom in his hand, he knew that it was going to be a long night.

Melissa closed her eyes and pulled him down to her, then she let out a throaty little laugh.

'You know, I'm told it's better if we both have our clothes off . . . unless you have something else in mind?'

She lay back and watched while he pulled off his boots and took off his clothes.

'Oh my,' she said, admiring his muscular form. 'Aren't you something?'

Halliday stretched out beside her with the bed-springs creaking under his weight.

'You don't know what it's been like for me in this dismal little hole of a town,' she whispered, nibbling his ear. 'Nobody does. I've felt like a prisoner. I have to get out, Buck!'

'Let's talk about that in morning. . . .'

Melissa seemed to have forgotten time and place and anything other than the wild craving that drove her to him. She pressed against him with every part of her body straining to bring him closer. Her hair fell across his face like silk. Her perfume touched his senses like lilacs on a hot spring night. There was too much woman here to deny, and too many lonely trails behind him.

He would have her, and he would have her now.

But Buck Halliday was still the man he'd always been. The gun was close by. His ears still listened for a sound that might mean danger from the place beyond their passion. . . .

When Buck Halliday finally moved away from her, Melissa's fingers lingered on his arm and then moved up his neck to hold him close. She was sleepy, but her body yearned for more.

'Please stay, Buck,' she whispered. 'I want you to make love to me again.'

'I'd best go.'

'No, Buck. Please don't go. You've got to stay.'

'Not now,' he said.

For just a moment, a look of hurt crossed her features and her eyes turned cold.

As Halliday got to his feet, dressed and buckled on his gunbelt, he thought of saying something more. He looked down at her for a moment and then he walked to the door and pulled back the bolt.

When he opened the door, Finch Rogan was only inches in front of him with his hand reaching for the knob.

'Buck?' Rogan said. 'What the hell. . . ?'

'Howdy, Finch,' Halliday said, moving slightly and giving Rogan a clear view into the room.

His face went white with the shock of what he saw. Then he eased his arm out of the sling.

'We could go get drunk and talk about old times,' Halliday said softly, 'or I guess you could try to kick my head in. . . .'

Halliday saw the awkward punch coming and easily dodged the blow. Then he simply stood Rogan back against the door and stepped around him.

When he saw Rogan clawing for his gun, he slapped his palm down hard on the man's wrist and the gun fell to the floor with a thump.

Rogan still had his eyes on the weapon, and when he moved toward it, Halliday kicked it away and planted a solid punch on the point of Rogan's jaw.

Rogan rocked on his feet and would have fallen, but Halliday caught him and helped him into the room.

When Melissa saw that he intended to lay Rogan on the bed, she jumped up and hastily wrapped herself in the crumpled skirt that lay on the floor.

'Get out! Get the hell out!'

'You knew he'd come,' Halliday said. 'So why did you want me to stay?'

'It was all your doing, Mr Halliday,' she said icily. 'You forced yourself on me.'

'I've seen my share of loose women,' Halliday said slowly, 'but I don't think I've ever come across one like you!'

'And I've never had a worse lover,' she said, her eyes blazing with anger. 'Call me a loose woman, but I think that's better than being called a fool! That's what you are, Halliday. So who do you think people are going to believe – you or me?'

Rogan stirred on the bed, and after another sour look at Melissa, Halliday backed out of the room and closed the door. He went along the passageway and returned to his room.

Melissa was right, of course. With even Rogan against him, he was in a town full of enemies. He was a fool.

He was also bone-tired. And not of a mind to run away with his tail between his legs.

Again he took off his boots and let them drop to the floor. Again he kept his gun beside him as he stretched out on the bed.

He could still smell the sweet scent of Melissa's body as he turned onto his side and went to sleep.

FIVE

RIDE ROUGHSHOD

Buck Halliday left the rooming house early the next morning, carrying his gear with him to the livery stable where he left it in the care of the stable hand.

He returned to the main street and was about to go down the alley beside the bank when he spotted Tom Mahoney coming from one end of town and Sheriff Luther Hahn from the other.

Mahoney looked remarkably buoyant, while Hahn was scowling.

Having no business with either of them, Halliday stepped into the alley and went around to the back of the bank. He knocked on the door and stood back to wait, rolling himself a cigarette.

It was Finch Rogan who opened the door, and when he saw Halliday, his face took on the look of somebody who had just been assaulted by a particularly foul odor.

'Come here to gloat, did you?' Rogan snarled.

'No. I came to talk.'

'I've got nothing to say to you, mister – not now, not ever again. If I was in better shape, I guess I'd at least have to try to cut you down.'

Halliday drew on his cigarette and studied his friend from behind a cloud of smoke.

'You wouldn't try, Finch. We've been through too much together for us to finish up like that.'

Rogan's eyes sparked with anger.

'Dammit, Buck, you can say that after what you did last night? I'd have killed you right then and there if I'd been able. I sure as hell tried. But I guess I should have known better, huh? You always were more than a match for me.'

'You've got a few things wrong, Finch,' Halliday said.

Rogan glared at him and laughed scornfully.

'I sure as hell have,' he said. 'What I've mainly got wrong is my impression of you as a man. I made my big mistake, but, by Judas, I won't make anymore. If you keep messing with Melissa's affections, I'll come after you. If I can't win, I'll damn well die trying. Now get away from me and stay away!'

The two men were eyeing each other in angry silence when Tom Mahoney came striding into the yard. The rancher smiled and said;

'Howdy, gents. Now ain't this a helluva fine mornin'? I'll tell you one thing – I hardly slept a wink last night and I never felt better. I was just like a kid waitin' to open his Christmas presents.'

Halliday saw Rogan's face change from anger to grim resignation. After a bitter glance at Halliday, Rogan turned to Mahoney and said;

'Come on in. Might as well get this damn day started and done with.'

'You ain't changed your mind about what you said last night, have you?' Mahoney asked quickly.

'Things have a way of changing, Tom, whether we like it or not. I said to come and see me. I had hopes of being able to help you by drawing on the resources of a certain friend of mine. But between last night and this morning, that idea blew up in my face. The upshot is that I've got no money for you.'

Mahoney's face fell, and then he turned to Halliday and looked at him curiously.

'Were you that certain friend?'

Halliday shook his head. 'No. But if I did have that kinda money, you could have first call on it.'

Mahoney returned his attention to Rogan.

'Who was it then? Hell, you made the offer, and I been thinkin' of nothin' else ever since. I can't last without that loan, Rogan, and you know it. I'm beggin' you. It's the first time I've ever had to beg in my whole life.'

Rogan shook his head.

'There's nothing I can do, Tom, and I'm sorry. I've dragged together every cent I could find, and there just isn't anymore. If it'd just damn well rain, we'd all be able to fight our way out of this mess. Without that, well, I just don't know what to say. . . .'

'McPhee's the one that's gonna bring us all down, ain't he?' Mahoney said sourly. 'He's the one that stopped me from shippin' my beef out so's I could get a decent price, and now he's the one that's gonna make you foreclose on all of us . . . ain't that right, Rogan?'

Rogan shot a sidelong glance at Halliday, who leaned uncomfortably against the back wall of the bank, dragging calmly on his cigarette. Then he said;

'I'm not at liberty to divulge the name of any business associate who has in the course of—'

'Associate be damned!' Mahoney snapped. 'That lowdown skunk has me by the throat, and he's chokin' the life outta me. I came to this territory willin' to work and go through hard times. I've had more than my share of that and I never once complained. But, by hell, I don't intend to go down without fightin' to the last breath of my body. So you give me a name, Rogan – I'll know it by tomorrow, anyway, so what's the difference?'

Rogan sighed and fiddled with the sling on his arm.

'Yeah,' he said slowly. 'It's Harp McPhee, all right. I borrowed a lot of money from him. I had to give him the mortgages on your place to do it, Tom. I had nowhere else to turn, and I didn't think for one minute that he was only investing in the bank so he could acquire a monopoly in these parts. I know now that I made a mistake. What happened to you at the freight yards proves it. I'm mighty sorry, Tom, but there's nothing I can do.'

Halliday watched Mahoney's shoulders slump as the old rancher turned and shuffled away without another word.

'Well, Halliday, that's all thanks to you,' Rogan said bitterly. 'You ruined the only chance there was to save that feller and through him, a lot of other folks around here. Unless you can think of some way to do some more damage, I figure it's about time you rode away and left us to our misery.'

'It isn't that simple, and you know it,' Halliday said flatly. 'You got in over your head, Finch. With this banking business and with Melissa, too. As for leavin' town, I'll decide when I'll go.'

He could still hear Rogan cussing him as he turned into the main street. Ahead of him, Mahoney was trudging in the direction of the saloon with the dragging footsteps of an old man.

The front door was closed, but Mahoney went around the side and Halliday followed him inside.

'I'm buyin', Tom,' Halliday said as they breasted the bar.

Mahoney shot a glance at him and made no reply.

To Halliday, the old rancher had the look of a man who had already given up.

Halliday took the money from his pocket and laid it on the counter. The barkeep served them and stood where he was until Halliday looked his way. With some reluctance, the man picked up his cleaning rag and wandered away.

'Don't be too hard on Finch,' Halliday said as they tasted their whiskey.

'Let me down, didn't he?' Mahoney grunted.

'In the end, yes, he did. But I know he meant to help you last night. It was just that what he had in mind didn't pan out.'

'What he had in mind last night was makin' himself look good. Why the hell did he have to raise my hopes like he did? I'm finished now.'

There was a crack in the old man's voice, and he looked quickly away.

'Plumb finished,' he repeated, and then he downed the remains of his drink in one long swallow.

Halliday could think of nothing more to say, so he simply bought them both another shot and let his mind run over his own worries.

So far, there was no sign of Luther Hahn. Halliday had expected the sheriff would be coming after him with blood in his eye. He wondered if Melissa would simply keep quiet or whether she would spin her father a story about how she had been dishonored by big, bad Buck Halliday. His hand strayed to his shirt pocket. The note was still there in case he needed to prove that Melissa had invited him to her room.

He still could not understand what game the woman was playing. It seemed certain that she had expected Rogan to appear on the scene all along.

Maybe she was just one of those women who liked to see men fight over her, but Halliday didn't think that was the case.

It was something else, something more complicated. There were all the signs that the whole sorry business had been planned in advance . . . but why?

Minutes passed, and the oldster maintained a stony silence.

Halliday was about to take a walk to the livery to check on the sorrel, but as he turned to go, he saw Harp McPhee come into the saloon by the back way.

McPhee glanced at Halliday, but it was clear that he had come to see Mahoney.

He ordered a drink and waited until he had the glass in his hand before he approached the rancher.

'Mahoney,' he said flatly, 'I hear you're in some difficulty.'

Mahoney's face flushed with anger and he stepped back from the bar so quickly that he almost stumbled. Then he turned on McPhee and rasped;

'You heard, did you? Don't act like it comes as a surprise, mister. This is all your doin', and I ain't never gonna forget it.'

There was no change in McPhee's expression. He

took a sip of his drink and set the glass down as if it disappointed him.

'Like I said last night, it's business. And nothing's happened to make me change my mind. I loaned Rogan a lot of money, and he gave me mortgages for security. Now it turns out the bank can't pay me what it owes me. That means I take over the mortgages. You can't expect me to just say goodbye to what's owin' to me, now can you?'

'I expect nothin' from you,' Mahoney spat.

'Now just hold on a minute and stop burnin' all your damn bridges, Tom,' McPhee countered. 'I'm a reasonable man and I'm prepared to help you out . . . if you want my help.'

'How?' Mahoney said contemptuously. 'With that damn fool offer you made last night?'

'Fool offer?' McPhee said with a faint grin. 'I don't see how you can call me a fool when I'm the only one around here that hasn't gone broke. That isn't somethin' I mean to change, either, but I'm still willin' to loan you another thousand dollars to meet the note the bank has against your place.'

Mahoney eyed him with distaste.

'Why? And what's in it for you?'

McPhee shrugged his big shoulders and smiled openly.

'Money, naturally. The interest on a loan has to be bigger when the risk is bad, you know. . . .'

'Go to hell and stay there!' Mahoney snapped.

79

'Get your damn stink outta here!'

McPhee still took no offense.

'Do it my way and you get to stay on your place for another three months,' he said. 'If it rains before the time is up, you might save enough of your cattle to pull you through. If it goes that way, you can pay back what you owe me and everybody comes away happy.'

'What the hell do you take me for – some kinda halfwit?' Mahoney barked.

'No, Tom,' McPhee said, 'not at all. I just take you for a man on his last legs.'

Halliday spoke for the first time.

'It's a bad deal, Tom,' he said.

McPhee spread his hands.

'That's the way life is a lot of the time,' he said. 'Now please, leave us alone so we can come to a decision.'

'I've already come to mine,' Mahoney muttered, knocking over his glass as he lunged at McPhee.

For a big man, Harp McPhee was quick on his feet. He stepped neatly out of the way, but the buttons on the cuff of his coat sleeve dragged for a moment on the edge of the bar.

Halliday saw the wrist gun and so did Mahoney, who stopped dead in his tracks.

'Just a precaution against hotheads,' McPhee said softly. 'But no matter, I'm sure you will learn to control yourself. Why don't you come back and get yourself another drink? My offer still stands, you know. You can have three months of hope ... or years of misery.'

Mahoney stepped back, and Halliday saw the anguish in his eyes. He knew that this time, the rancher was down for the count and it was all going according to plan for McPhee. Just as it had also done last night, when Melissa went straight from McPhee to the rooming house and into Halliday's arms. That had to be another plan. Or part of the same plan that was dragging the whole town to the edge of ruin ...

'McPhee,' Halliday said, 'you're ridin' this town too hard, and your turn's coming.'

McPhee's smile faded.

'Is that supposed to be some kind of threat?'

'No, you ain't worth that, mister. You'll get yours soon enough, and when the time comes, nothin's going to help you – not your foolish little sneak gun or your hired gun or anything else you got to protect you from the decent folks who've had a bellyful of you.

'Just do like Sheriff Hahn said and git!'

McPhee's mouth worked soundlessly for a time before he pulled his sleeve down to cover the wrist gun. Glancing quickly around the room, he stepped back from the bar.

Jeff Leonard and four other businessmen were just coming in the door, and they looked at him with hatred as they crossed to the bar.

McPhee turned back to Mahoney then and raised his voice in a way that made it clear he was addressing everyone in the room.

'When I make a deal, I stick to it,' he said. 'I expect everybody else to do likewise. If they don't, too bad . . . for them.'

Leonard's head swung around angrily, and one of his companions made a point of projecting a thin stream of tobacco juice onto the floor only inches from McPhee's shiny boots.

'None of that's going to change a thing,' McPhee said, and then he sauntered across the room and out the door, leaving the batwings trembling behind his back.

Mahoney muttered a curse, but Halliday touched him on the shoulder and said;

'Gettin' mad can only do you more harm than good, Tom.'

'I know that,' the rancher growled.

There was a short silence before he spoke again.

'Somethin' I don't know, though. . . .'

'And what might that be?' Halliday asked casually.

'I can't figure why you're still here. Why buy into this mess when it's got nothin' at all to do with you?'

'You've got a point,' Halliday said. 'I'm kinda wondering the same thing myself . . . but I figure you'd do what you could if you were in my place. McPhee seems to affect everybody the same way. He just about turns my stomach.'

'He does at that,' Mahoney mumbled, reaching for his drink.

Halliday leaned back against the counter and glanced at Leonard and his friends. The strain was showing in all their faces. This was a town with no joy, and only one man was responsible.

The barkeep was working his way back down the bar, leaving a damp smear on the countertop with his rag. His eyes kept darting in Halliday's direction as though he expected some kind of mayhem to erupt at any minute.

His apprehension seemed to grow when Luther Hahn looked in over the batwings and then sauntered inside.

When the sheriff left soon afterward without incident, Halliday was every bit as surprised as the bartender.

A few more customers ambled in, paid for their drinks and settled into their usual places.

Halliday decided that it was just another ordinary day – for a town that was slowly dying on its feet.

He drained his glass and set it down, and then he turned to face Mahoney and extended his hand.

'Well, Tom,' he said, 'I've had enough of Redemption. I'm on my way. I hope somethin' turns up for you.'

Mahoney reached for Halliday's hand and shook it firmly.

'It's a shame there's nothin' to keep you here,' he

said. 'In better times, I reckon we would have worked damn well together.'

'No doubt about that,' Halliday said as he tilted his hat brim in preparation for stepping into the bright sunlight outside.

He was turning to go when the batwings creaked again.

Wes Rudder stood just inside the room, scanning the drinkers slowly until his eyes found Halliday.

There was no trace now of that faintly mocking grin. The lean, dark face was set like stone, and both hands were hooked in the double gunrig.

'Glad you ain't run off, Halliday,' Rudder said in a voice that carried to every corner of the suddenly silent room. 'Too hot a day to have to hunt you down.'

No one moved. All eyes watched the beginning of what looked like a drama of life and death. Halliday saw Mahoney stir beside him and said;

'Stay out of it, Tom.'

Then he moved slightly toward Rudder, regarding him with a steady look that refused any distraction.

'I don't run, mister, and you sure ain't the man to make me start.'

Rudder's lips peeled back in a snarl.

'You got good reason to run, mister. Real good.'

'I do?'

Rudder thumped his chest.

'I'm it, Halliday. From the time you bought into

that business at the freight yards, I've been strainin' at the bit. Now you've gone too far, the way you talked to Mr McPhee. You shoulda shown him more respect . . .'

'I'm not much good at pretending,' Halliday said slowly, 'and respect just doesn't come easy when a man's looking at a cockroach like Harp McPhee.'

Mahoney shifted noisily away from the bar.

'Now just a damn minute,' he said. 'Halliday never said a thing to McPhee. It was me that called him scum and tried to take a swing at him. I shoulda known that even with that sneak gun up his sleeve, it'd come to nothin' and he'd send you to fight his battle for him.'

Rudder heard the little rancher out, then rasped;

'Like Halliday said, stay outta this.'

Without taking his eyes from the gunman, Halliday gave a barely perceptible nod and motioned Mahoney to step away.

'I'll get Hahn,' Mahoney said. 'We ain't standin' by and seein' you cut down an innocent man, Rudder. We ain't about to let you call the tune on this.'

'Back off, Tom,' Halliday told the rancher gently. 'This has nothin' to do with you or Luther Hahn.'

He stepped into the center of the room, still facing Rudder.

'Still mighty sure of yourself, ain't you?' Rudder sneered in an attempt to goad Halliday into making a wrong move.

85

'Sure enough, mister. I don't see anything to change my mind.'

Rudder's face did not alter, but there was an almost imperceptible change in his eyes.

Halliday saw it and knew that Rudder was about to go for his gun. He waited with his hands hanging loosely at his sides.

Both men heard the faint scrape of feet at the back of the room. Rudder was the first to look that way, and then Halliday cut his gaze in the same direction.

Melissa Hahn was standing there, with Harp McPhee beside her, leaning against the wall.

A moment later, Luther Hahn marched into the room without giving a glance to either his daughter or Harp McPhee. He stood there with his feet planted wide and his chin jutting out aggressively as his eyes swept over the room and then settled on the two men who were facing each other down.

'Buyin' in on this, are you, Hahn?' Rudder inquired.

Luther Hahn shook his head.

'Nope,' he said. 'The way I heard it, Halliday tried to lean on Mr McPhee. You work for McPhee, so I reckon you got a right to act on his behalf – just so's it's a fair fight, of course.'

Hahn moved a little closer to the bar and studied Jeff Leonard and his companions, and then he turned slowly and ran his eyes over the rest of the customers.

'The rest of you, keep your noses outta this,' the lawman commanded. 'Halliday killed a man in the street as soon as he rode into this town, and he's been makin' trouble ever since, but he ain't done nothin' I can jail him for. If Wes wants to take care of this, that's fine by me.'

Hahn nodded in Rudder's direction and the gunslick returned the gesture. Halliday set his feet and fixed his attention completely on the gunman facing him.

'Well, Rudder,' he said quietly, 'you called it, so I guess you'd best get on with it.'

Without taking his attention away from Rudder, Halliday sensed that Melissa had moved away from McPhee's side. He knew then that she would be trying to get a better view of what was probably the most exciting event in her life.

Rudder's whole body went rigid. There was not a single sound in the room.

Mahoney was watching Halliday and thinking that this was no longer the man he had come to count as a friend. This was the stranger he had seen for the first time at the railroad siding – the man with no friends other than the gun on his hip.

When it came, Rudder's draw was smooth and fast. His teeth flashed in something that was almost a smile. He was so sure that Halliday was yet another who could not match that lightning draw.

Then he saw the gun in Halliday's hand, and the

bullet had shattered something in his chest and knocked him sideways before his finger touched the trigger.

The bullet meant for Halliday smashed into the wall a yard from Luther Hahn.

The sheriff jumped and swore and then looked around quickly to see who in the room may have noticed his fear.

Rudder was still on his feet and glaring at Halliday with the hatred of a beaten man. He shook his head in disbelief and muttered something no one could hear. A trickle of blood ran down his chin, and he compressed his lips in a thin line as though he was scared of dying.

Nobody moved. Nobody spoke.

Rudder began to fall to one side but everything in him strained to keep him on his feet. He seemed to be suspended, like a puppet hanging from slack strings. Then whatever puppeteer guided a man like Wes Rudder simply discarded him.

The killer had been killed.

Everyone knew by the way he fell that McPhee's hired gun was dead.

'Judas!' Mahoney whispered hoarsely, and then there was a murmur of many voices.

'They both drew so fast I never even seen it!'

'I figured Rudder got his gun out first, didn't you?'

'What's McPhee gonna do now?'

'I'll never be able to come in here again without I

remember this . . .'

Then Halliday holstered his gun and turned toward the back of the saloon.

The silence descended as heavy as a deluge.

The sheriff, Melissa and McPhee were bunched close together by the back door, and Halliday had them transfixed in a gaze as cold as winter snow.

'You better be damn sure to call this the way it was,' he said. 'Too many other folks saw it for you to try anything else.'

Halliday began to back toward the batwings, his gun hand loose at his side near the holster.

Hahn was scowling and breathing noisily through his nose like an enraged bull, but Melissa was the first of the spectators to make a move. She let out a cry and broke into a run. McPhee reached for her but was too late to stop her from running to what was left of a gunman who had finally met his match.

SIX

NO DUST,
NO DISTANCE

Tom Mahoney followed Buck Halliday out onto the boardwalk, and then turned and stood on his toes to take one last look over the batwings.

He saw Melissa Hahn cradling Wes Rudder's head on her lap, her face smeared with his blood where she had kissed him.

'Judas,' the old rancher said in wonderment, 'everybody figured she was gonna get hitched up with Finch. . . .'

Halliday wasn't listening. He was watching the banker rushing toward the saloon.

'What have you done now?' Finch Rogan asked bitterly as he reached Halliday.

'See for yourself,' Halliday told him.

'What you gonna do now, son?' Mahoney asked softly when Rogan had gone.

'Well,' Halliday said with a ghost of a grin, 'I'd get myself a drink if that wasn't the only saloon in town.'

'I don't suppose you want my advice,' Mahoney said, 'but if you did, I'd say get the hell out of this hole and don't come back. You don't owe this town a damn thing, and it's clear that damn near everybody is in on what's goin' on, includin' the sheriff and maybe Finch Rogan, too.'

Halliday shrugged and said, 'Maybe you're right at that, Tom. If I hear you got rain in time for it to do you any good, I might come back and give you a hand with the drive.'

'The easiest trail out is toward Moondance,' Mahoney said, pointing the direction with a stubby finger.

Halliday nodded and headed for the alley by the saloon, on his way to the stables.

He was just turning the corner when he heard the creak of the batwings at the front door to the saloon. The next thing he heard was Finch Rogan's voice and light footsteps on the boardwalk behind him.

Melissa Hahn was running at him with her hair flying and her arms outstretched. He grabbed her as she rushed at him with her nails tearing at his face, and he held her at arm's length as she kicked and scratched with all the ferocity of a wildcat.

Halliday looked past her and saw Rogan and Hahn rushing toward him.

When Rogan reached him and grabbed his shoulder, Halliday shook him off and snapped;

'Ain't you ever gonna learn? Can't you see they've made a fool out of you?'

'No!' Rogan hissed. 'All I've learned is how you treat your friends. I'll never forgive you for what you did to Melissa.'

'Then you're even more of a fool than I thought!' Halliday snapped, and then he cursed as Melissa got past his guard and he felt the sharp sting of her nails raking his cheek.

Shoving the woman away with one hand, he lashed out with his fist and connected neatly with Rogan's jaw. The hard shove lifted Melissa off her feet and forced her back.

With a grunt of surprise and effort, her father saved her from falling and then fastened a strong grip on her arm. The sheriff studied his daughter grimly for a moment, and then he asked;

'Is it true then, what McPhee said inside?'

Melissa tried to pull away from him, but Hahn hung on until she finally went quiet.

'Yes, pa,' she said. 'He broke into my room and forced himself on me.'

Rogan was up and coming back for more, but Halliday stepped aside and let him charge on past.

'Dammit, Finch!' Halliday protested. 'Can't you

wait long enough to get the facts straight?'

'I got all the facts I need, you skunk!' Rogan shouted. 'And, by hell, I won't quit until I kill you—'

Halliday hit him with a hard right and a left upper-cut.

Rogan cried out when his bandaged shoulder hit the wall. He slid to his knees and stayed there, clutching at his shoulder. His face was so white that it seemed he was about to faint.

Luther Hahn had been waiting his turn. Now he pushed his daughter behind him and advanced on Halliday.

'OK, mister,' he said thickly, 'you've had your fun in this town. Now we'll have ours.'

Halliday squared himself to face him, but then he saw that Hahn was going for his gun. For one brief moment, he expected he would have to draw on the sheriff to defend himself. He knew what that would mean – running fast and far, with a price on his head.

Halliday had forgotten all about Tom Mahoney, but now the old rancher was stepping into the thick of it with his six-gun drawn.

'Hold it, Hahn,' Mahoney said in a calm, deter-mined voice. 'This has gone just as far as it's goin' to.'

Hahn turned on the rancher, and his face was livid with anger. 'Keep out of this, Mahoney!' he shouted.

'I been in it all along,' Mahoney said, 'ever since McPhee decided to force me off my ranch. Halliday's about the only one to stick up for me, and I'm damned if I'm gonna see him suffer for it. McPhee tried to get him with his hired gun. That didn't work, and now here's the goddamn law, tryin' its best to do McPhee's biddin'. You call yourself a sheriff . . . you oughtta be ashamed of yourself, Luther.'

'I'm warnin' you, Mahoney,' Hahn began, taking a step toward the old rancher. 'You been another thorn in my side for too long . . .'

'Do what you like,' Mahoney challenged, 'but first, why don't you explain why you stood back and waited while Rudder prodded this feller here into a gunfight. You was just hopin' Rudder would gun Halliday down, weren't you?'

'I'll tell you nothin', you old buzzard!' Hahn snapped. 'Get that gun off me.'

Mahoney shook his head and stood his ground, his fierce determination showing in his weather-beaten features. The old man flicked a look Halliday's way and told him;

'Best get goin', Buck. I'll be fine once these gutless wonders know they can't get at you.'

Halliday turned a thoughtful look on Rogan, who was getting shakily to his feet. He reached out to Melissa for support, but she stepped away from him and folded her arms.

'Stay away from me, you fool!' Melissa snapped. 'I can't stand for you to touch me.'

Rogan gaped at her and then shook his head as though he did not believe his ears.

'Hell, Melissa,' he muttered, 'you and me were—'

'You fool!' Melissa said again, and then she went to stand beside her father. Turning to face Halliday, she said, 'Don't you think for one minute that this is finished. I don't care where you go, we'll find you. Wes has a lot of friends. They'll hunt you down and kill you.'

Halliday started to walk away, and that was when the shot rang out from the rooftop of the saloon.

Then Tom Mahoney's gun flew out of his hand and he was reeling back with blood streaming from a furrow in his forehead. Halliday saw the sheriff use the commotion to go for his gun, but he still managed to beat the lawman to the draw. When he saw Hahn drag the hammer back with his thumb, he fired and got the lawman's gun hand. Hahn yelped and staggered sideways into his daughter, knocking her off her feet.

Melissa was screaming and Hahn was roaring with anger, but another burst of gunfire silenced them both.

This time, someone was firing from the doorway of the saloon.

Halliday turned with the six-gun smoking in his hand as his eyes searched for the gunman, but now there was no one in the doorway.

Leonard and a few others had come running, and now they were clustered around Mahoney as he lay on the ground.

'Git out while you can, Buck,' Mahoney said hoarsely, but Halliday was running for the batwings where the last shot had been fired.

A bullet tore a hole through Halliday's shirt, burning across his chest. He glanced up in time to see the man on the roof, a small man entirely intent on edging back from the false front. Halliday lined him up in his sights and allowed for the angle. He fired only once, and the man pitched face-forward against the corrugated iron and then came sliding down the metal and thudded into the street.

Halliday hurried back to Mahoney and was relieved to see that the old rancher was on his feet again and holding a bandanna to his head.

Rogan, Hahn and Melissa were still there but all standing at a distance from one another like they'd been in a heated argument.

'I guess that's about it, Hahn,' Halliday told the lawman who was nursing a broken hand. 'You tried to do your best by Harp McPhee, but it just didn't come out right, did it? When he comes out of hidin', tell him he'll get more than he bargained for if he keeps on the way he's been doin'.'

Easing Mahoney along in front of himself, Halliday started for the alley.

'Halliday,' Hahn rasped, 'I'm chargin' you with murder.'

'Of him?' Halliday asked, jerking his chin at the dead man in the street.

'Yeah,' Hahn said grimly. 'Will Cross was only doin' his duty by this town, protectin' a lawman from assault by that old coot. You killed him, mister, and you'll hang for it.'

Halliday shook his head.

'I don't think so. I sure don't see anybody here that's good enough to put a rope around my neck. Do you?'

Halliday gave Mahoney a gentle push and then looked back at Rogan.

The banker held his stare but said nothing.

'Some other time, Finch,' Halliday said as he followed Mahoney into the alley.

Both the rancher and Halliday collected their horses, and then Mahoney led the way out of town – the back way.

'This sure is a town for backshooters,' Halliday answered as they rode away.

Harp McPhee was pacing the room and cussing to himself in a steady mumble. Every time he looked up at his company, the cussing intensified.

With his gun hand bandaged, Luther Hahn stood against the wall like an overgrown school kid sent to stand in the corner.

Covered by a stained horse blanket, the body of McPhee's hired gun lay on a table at the end of the room.

Crying fit to break her heart, Melissa grieved over

the failed gunfighter.

'What a useless bunch,' McPhee said in disgust, and then his attention settled on Melissa and he said, 'Can't you stop that caterwaulin'? Have I got to put up with that, too?'

Melissa continued to wail, and McPhee went on pacing the floor.

'Nice mess we're in, thanks to that second-rate gunman,' he said tightly. 'You told me Wes Rudder was the best, Luther. Remember?'

'I figured he was,' Hahn said in a subdued voice. 'Down on the Platte, they reckon—'

'This ain't the Platte, dammit! This is Redemption. I've done everything right so far, except for pickin' the people to work with. You had Halliday and you let him get away.'

'I wasn't the only one that messed up, and you know it,' Hahn protested. 'How come you missed him from the saloon? That should've been a real easy shot, and he sure was a clear target.'

'I'm not a gunman,' McPhee scowled. 'That's why I shell out good money for men like Rudder . . . and you.'

He went on walking until he came to the window, and then he pounded his fist on the sill in sheer frustration.

Hahn wiped his face with his sleeve and inspected his bandaged hand again.

Then McPhee put his back to the window and said

more quietly, 'Well, there's no sense in blamin' each other . . . and cryin' over what's gone. What we need to do now is take stock of how we stand. What do you reckon about the folks in town?'

'How do you mean, Mr McPhee?'

'I mean how they feel about us. Your girl played a pretty fair hand for awhile, but Halliday was wise to her. Then—'

'Yeah,' Hahn interrupted, glaring at his daughter. 'My girl played a pretty fair hand for somebody layin' on her back – by hell, Melissa, if your ma could see what you've been up to, I don't know what she'd say!'

'She would have understood,' Melissa snapped. 'She would have thought the same way, felt the same way and acted the same way.'

Hahn strode across the room and slapped his daughter hard across the face.

'I reckon I shoulda done that a long time ago, before you had a chance to make a fool of me in front of the whole damn town,' the sheriff snarled at her. 'Now set there quiet, dammit. We've got worries of our own.'

'The biggest worry I have right now is you,' McPhee admitted. 'And getting in touch with Bob Rudder and telling him he can have his brother's job if he wants it. If he says no, I guess you better start doing some target practice with your one good hand. The thing is, I don't reckon we've seen the last of Halliday, and we have to be ready for him.'

Hahn sucked in a long breath.

'That's a pretty tall order,' he said.

'We're not playin' some penny-ante game here. This is high stakes – mighty high. The first thing you have to do is get a fresh grip on this town. You tell folks whatever you want, but just make sure they don't get any fancy ideas about standin' up to me. If a few of them start to step out of line, it could be they'll be too hard to handle. I've figured everything out so it's legal, but that won't be all it takes unless you come down hard on anybody with a mind to argue. We did a good job of bustin' Rogan, but we can't stop now.'

McPhee picked up his hat and headed for the door, stopping on his way to pat Melissa on the shoulder.

'Don't take on so, little lady,' he comforted her. 'You just do what I ask of you, and I'll see that you're looked after. Who knows? It might even be that the two of us could get together once this is over. . . .'

Melissa gave him a speculative look, and seeing the expression on her face, her father cursed her.

'You goddamn alley cat,' he muttered.

McPhee shot him a severe look, and Hahn stormed out of the room.

When he'd gone, McPhee turned back to her and regarded her thoughtfully.

'You think about it, Melissa – about us gettin' together. It might work out.'

His eyes ran up and down her body and Melissa

tossed her head.

'I don't know,' she pouted. 'You never showed much interest in me before.'

McPhee laid a hand on her shoulder again and held it firmly.

'I could give you lots of pretty things, and good times in big towns – maybe even back East. I always figured Rudder was too rough for a gal like you. I reckon I could give you just about anything you'd ever want.'

Melissa's eyes gleamed with a new excitement.

'A big house and servants to look after it?' she said.

'Not till it's all over, Melissa, like you said. Just so you do what I ask,' McPhee emphasized.

He left her standing at the door watching him go. Harp McPhee might have had his worries, but no one would have known it from his jaunty stride.

He had the liveryman hitch his horses to the rig, and then he started off in the noonday heat. When the liveryman remarked that it was too hot to move, McPhee only smiled and said;

'Business is business, mister, and it doesn't wait for cooler weather.'

His first call was on the widow Mary Harper, who stood on her front porch with three children peeking shyly from behind her dusty skirts.

Squinting into the glare of the sun coming over McPhee's shoulder, she gave the man a reluctant greeting.

McPhee removed his hat and mopped his brow with a wadded bandanna as he smiled at her.

'Did you do what I asked?' he said.

The woman pursed her lips and looked away.

'I just couldn't, Mr McPhee. Tom has always been a friend to this family, and a real good neighbor.'

'He's beat, ma'am,' McPhee said. 'Now you can be beat with him or not. Suit yourself.'

She shook her head again and said, 'I can't do it.'

'Well, then, you better start packin',' McPhee said sternly.

A curly-haired little girl began to toy with her mother's apron, but the woman slapped her hand away. The round face reddened and a fat tear formed in her eye. Then the mother was crying, too.

'This place is all we have,' she said, 'and it surely cannot be much use to you. There's nothin' here but dust and loneliness. The well's about to run dry, and everythin' in the garden's burned up in the heat. Please, Mr McPhee, just leave us be.'

'All you have to do to stay on here is tell the sheriff that Mahoney ran off your cows, ma'am. Sheriff Hahn will do the rest,' McPhee said soothingly. 'Do that, and you get to keep your place, mortgage free, and maybe I'll even throw in some stock when the drought breaks. You got three nice children there, ma'am, don't they mean more to you than Tom Mahoney?'

'They do,' she exploded tearfully, 'they're all that matters.'

'Well then, you know what you have to do.'

'I can't lie,' she insisted.

'Then I guess you better get ready to watch these brats of yours starve. You sleep on it, Mrs Harper. I'll be back in the mornin'.'

The woman pushed her children into the house and closed the door behind them. Then she quickly followed McPhee to his rig, noticing with something like wonder that the buggy was so highly polished that the dust could hardly settle on it and the horses were so fat and frisky that they seemed eager to run in the traces.

'You have Tom Mahoney down on his knees as it is,' she said. 'Why do you have to do this, too?'

'Not takin' any chances, ma'am,' he replied. 'Mahoney's given me plenty of trouble. He spoke against me after all I ever did was help him out. I can't be blamed for this drought, now, can I? Now you think some more about all this, and maybe you'll decide to let me be your friend.'

McPhee turned the rig and drove away, looking back just long enough to tip his hat.

The widow let out an exhausted sigh. It had been four lonely years since her man was shot, and the struggle had left its mark. She had kept going with the help of neighbors, to whom she could offer no repayment. The place was now mortgaged to the hilt and the money was all gone.

She stood there in the dusty yard for a long time,

looking blankly at the dead bush beside the gate. That rose had been her pride and joy, and the only thing that reminded her of a gracious life. The children had toted water to it faithfully, but now there was barely enough in the well for the family and the old horse and the last of the scraggly chickens.

When she finally turned back toward the house, there was more purpose in her step. She was thinking what her husband would have done to a skunk like Harp McPhee, but she was a woman after all – she would have to find another way to fight.

'Jimmy!' she called to her eldest boy. 'Get the trunk down from the loft in the barn, and then get the buckboard ready. You'd best feed the horse. We'll be leavin' soon.'

'Where we goin', ma?' the boy asked as he headed for the barn to hitch up the horse.

'To Red Rock,' she said. 'We're goin' to visit Aunt Thelma.'

SEVEN

THE MEETING

Tom Mahoney nursed his throbbing head and cussed at the inconvenience of it all. The pain itself did not worry him unduly, for he had been hurt too much in his life not to know that wounds healed in time and healed quicker if a man did not dwell on them.

He rode onto his own land in the middle of the afternoon, and almost at once, he and Buck Halliday spotted three horses loping toward them.

Mahoney stopped and shaded his eyes with his hand.

'Bosker, Milligan and Thomas,' he muttered. 'What the hell could they want?'

'I guess they'll tell us soon enough,' Halliday said, and then he reined – in beside Mahoney and waited for the three horsemen to reach them.

As the men came closer, Halliday saw that the three were ranchers with faces every bit as grim as Mahoney's. Then the old rancher introduced Halliday to his neighbors.

Cole Bosker studied Halliday for a minute or so, and then he asked, 'Are you the one that did for Wes Rudder?'

'He sure is,' Mahoney answered quickly. 'You heard about it already, huh?'

'Johnston from the Bar-Double-K happened by,' Bosker informed Mahoney. 'He said you were hurt and that a feller name of Halliday cut Rudder down. Said he tangled with Luther Hahn, too. That so?'

'In a way,' Halliday said in a noncommittal tone of voice.

Mahoney could see that Halliday was uneasy with the conversation.

'Well, Cole,' he said, 'I guess you folks didn't ride all this way to talk over news you heard already. . . .'

'No,' Bosker said. 'Come for another reason, Tom. We tried to see Finch Rogan, but he was havin' nothin' to do with us. So we went to see McPhee, and he offered us as hard a damned contract as I ever heard about.'

'I know all about that,' Mahoney said. 'Same thing happened to me.'

'So what'd you say to him?'

'I told him to go fry in hell.'

Bosker nodded and indicated his companions

with a jerk of his thumb.

'Same as us,' he said, 'but the thing is, we're just about beat. We had us a talk on the way back from town and figured we can do one of two things. We can let Rogan double-cross us and allow McPhee to take over, then we can pack up and move with our tails between our legs. Or we can fight.'

'Are you talkin' about a shootin' fight?' Mahoney asked.

All three nodded, and Milligan spoke for the first time.

'McPhee sure has asked for it. Rogan says we're just askin' for more trouble, but I don't see what we've got to lose.'

Mahoney's eyes gleamed with interest.

'Figured I was on my own in this,' he said. 'Until Buck here come along, I thought I'd just have to tackle Rudder and McPhee all by myself. Now the three of you are speakin' up . . . things are startin' to look hopeful.'

Mahoney flicked a quick glance Halliday's way, and asked;

'What do you reckon, Buck? Do you want some more excitement? Strikes me you ain't a man that walks away from a good fight!'

Halliday stayed silent for almost a minute, and then he looked at each of the ranchers in turn. He had intended to see Mahoney safely home and then head off for parts unknown, but now he was not so sure.

'I've got no fight with Finch Rogan,' he told them.

'Not after what he said to you back there in town?' Mahoney said with a frown. 'Hell, you take that kinda treatment from a polecat like Rogan, next thing—'

'He's no polecat,' Halliday said. 'He's just a feller that got in over his head. I talked this over with him yesterday. He knows he took a risk with McPhee, but he didn't have anybody else to turn to. And now McPhee's backed him into a corner. It stinks, but it's legal. Finch's tried every way he can to help you fellers get outta this mess – he was even hopin' to get some money from Melissa to bail Mahoney out until I got in the way.'

'How'd you do that? Hell, she's his woman. Everybody knows that. If she's got money, then maybe. . . .'

'Everybody thought she was his woman, especially Finch,' Halliday said. 'But it turned out she was messin' with Wes Rudder.'

Bosker's jaw dropped.

'The two of them?'

'It sure looked that way to me,' Mahoney put in. 'That gal near suffered a seizure when Rudder got what was comin' to him. Then she came after Buck with blood in her eye, and her pa bought in, and I'm tellin' you, there was one helluva ruckus.'

'You don't have to feel like you're at fault over Melissa,' Bosker said unexpectedly. 'There's more to that one than meets the eye.'

'All I'm saying,' Halliday told him, 'is that I wouldn't like anything to happen to Finch. His crime was bein' a mite foolish, but that's as far as it goes.'

Plainly puzzled by this turn of events, Mahoney straightened his back and addressed his neighbors.

'If you want to fight,' he said, 'you can count me in. Rudder's out of the way, and so are two other fellers. About the only one McPhee's got left is the sheriff, and Buck shattered his gun hand with a bullet.'

'Yeah?' Thomas asked, eyeing Halliday intently.

'It's true,' muttered Mahoney. 'I sure wish you'd stay awhile longer, Buck. I ain't trying to offend you none, but hell, every man has to make his way best he can. We can offer you a share in what we got if you can see your way clear to stickin' around and helpin' us. . . .'

'It wouldn't work,' Halliday told them flatly. 'The townsfolk would never go along with what you're proposin'. Maybe the law is a mite bent, but it's still the law and they aren't the kind to buck it. Take Jeff Leonard, for instance. If he was gonna do somethin', he would have made a move long before now.'

'No, he wouldn't,' Mahoney said quickly. 'Nothin' falls due till tomorrow. It just ain't hit home to him yet.'

Bosker grunted his agreement, and his two companions nodded also. Halliday looked out into the distance. The empty spaces called to him.

'Time we got you home, Tom,' was all he said.

'That all you got to say, Buck?' Mahoney scowled.

'I reckon it is, Tom. It's not my town, and it's not my land. You know damn well that I wouldn't take a cent for helpin' you. Money's not my main problem.'

'So what is?' Mahoney pressed.

'Finch Rogan,' Halliday said. 'The two of us rode some mighty hard trails together. He's not like everyone thinks he is. If you're grateful that I've helped you, I'd like to have your word that you'll leave Finch be.'

Mahoney looked quickly at the others. Bosker shrugged his shoulders and slapped at a fly.

'Cole?' Mahoney prodded.

'I just don't know if Halliday's right or wrong about Rogan,' Bosker said, 'but I guess I'll leave it to you, Tom.'

Mahoney nodded and chewed noisily on his bottom lip. Then he said;

'OK, you all head on home, but stop in on Watson and Smith on the way. We can all get together at my place first thing in the mornin' . . . and all head for Watson's place. That'll be where McPhee goes first.'

Halliday sensed that Mahoney was talking himself into doing something he would much rather avoid. He did not doubt that once committed, Mahoney would carry this thing through to the end and likely get himself killed.

He walked his sorrel up the slope and stopped on

the top of a rise. The parched land spread out in front of him looked no better than wasteland. Only fools would fight over a place like that – fools or people whose roots were sunk too deeply into the drought-stricken ground.

When his neighbors rode away, Mahoney brought his mount alongside Halliday's, and said;

'Well, it's time we went, too.'

'You know the law's on McPhee's side, don't you?' Halliday asked as they heeled their mounts into motion.

'I guess so,' Mahoney said, 'but he's doin' a bad thing, law or no law. Even if this is the last fight for me, I'm taking that tinhorn with me, Buck. It don't matter much to me at my age, but I figure I owe it to my neighbors. They're good men, and they've worked as hard as a man can to make somethin' out of their ranches. Bosker's always been willin' to fight for what's his, and Milligan, he's got a wife and kids who depend on him. Thomas ain't ever said a bad word against anybody until he came up against McPhee. I can't turn my back on them, Buck. It just wouldn't be right.'

They rode on in silence under the scorching sun. Finally, they reached Mahoney's fence, and Halliday opened the gate and let the old man through. Then he led the sorrel onto Mahoney's land and closed the gate.

The two men rode into the yard, side by side.

Mahoney's men came out to greet him, and when they saw the blood on his head, they tried to help him down from the saddle.

'I'm all right,' Mahoney said irritably. 'Just leave me be. Somebody can take these hosses and give 'em a feed, though. Look after the sorrel first – Buck's gonna be leavin' soon as he's had some grub and it gets a touch cooler.'

Halliday nodded gratefully. He expected that the sorrel could use all the special treatment it could get. It had been a long, hard ride to Redemption with little time so far to recover.

Even the slow ride to this ranch had tired the sorrel more than Halliday liked, and he was thinking he would have to baby it along for a few days more before it got its strength back.

Mahoney brought a half-bottle of whiskey out onto the porch, taking a swig and then passing the bottle from hand to hand as his cowpokes squatted with their backs against the railing.

It seemed to be a tacit admission that there was not much for a ranch hand to do on yet another hot, dry afternoon.

Halliday sat beside the old rancher and stared out into the distance. Mahoney and the cowpokes talked a little, but for the most part, there was a companionable silence.

Halliday was thinking about the difference between being lonesome and being alone. Most of the time, he preferred his own company, but Finch Rogan had been the rare exception – the kind of friend who was never demanding. It was a shame to bust up that kind of friendship, especially over a woman who did not seem to really want either of the former friends.

The day droned on, slow and silent as every living thing tried to conserve energy and stay out of the sun.

It started to change just before dusk. A wind whipped up out of nowhere, bringing a surprising chill with it.

The men on the porch began to stir, and one of them stepped off the porch and looked up at the sky. Mahoney watched him curiously, and finally asked;

'What's it doin', Jake?'

The cowpoke shook his head doubtfully.

'Damned if I know, boss. Almost feels like there might be a storm buildin'. . . .'

'Why don't you ride up the ridge and get a better look?' Mahoney suggested.

'Why the hell not?' Jake concurred.

He walked across the yard in his run-over boots, heading for the corral.

'It's somethin' havin' a wind to cool the place down, even if that's all there is to it,' Mahoney concluded.

'Somebody's comin',' one of the other men remarked with mild interest.

Everyone except for Halliday craned their necks to see who it was.

'That's two unusual things in a row,' Mahoney commented. 'Don't that look like Mrs Harper's buckboard?'

'Yeah, boss, and she's pushin' that old hoss mighty hard,' the cowpoke confirmed.

It took no effort to stop the heavily-loaded buckboard. As soon as the sad-eyed woman on the box seat let the reins go loose, the horse simply stopped and let its head droop.

Halliday counted three kids among the boxes and bundles in the flatbed.

'Looks like you've already made up your mind, Mary,' Mahoney said.

'I had to, Tom. McPhee paid me a visit today, and he tried to do a deal. Seems like the only way he'll let us stay is if I do somethin' bad. That old farm ain't worth much at all these days, and it sure isn't worth losin' good friends over it – so I figured it was time to go.'

Halliday saw Mahoney's face harden.

'What was it that skunk wanted you to do, Mary? By hell, if he was askin' you to—'

'No,' the woman said, dropping her eyes in embarrassment. 'It was nothin' like that. He wanted me to accuse you of rustlin' my cows.'

'Now who'd believe a crazy thing like that, even if he found somebody to say it?' Mahoney snorted.

'Not likely anybody would believe it, Tom,' the woman said, 'but he seemed to think it would be a help to have Luther charge you . . . but like I said, the ranch isn't worth enough to make me tell lies against a neighbor that's helped us hang on as long as we did. I guess maybe he thought it would take the attention away from what he's doin', foreclosin' on everybody, if you was jailed for rustlin'.'

Mahoney swore under his breath and slapped his hand down hard on the porch rail.

'That does it! That buzzard's asked for it, and now he's gonna get it!'

He went down the steps and stood by the buckboard to say farewell to the family.

'You're a fine woman, Mary,' he said, 'and these kids are a credit to you. I think you're doin' the right thing in gettin' out of here, at least for the time bein'. Gonna stay with your sister in Red Rock, are you?'

'Yes,' the woman said. 'It's the only thing that came to mind.'

'Well, you do that, but write to me in a week or so and tell me how you're gettin' on. I'll write back soon as there's somethin' to report, and let you know what's happenin'.'

Halliday felt sorry for the little family with nowhere to go, but he knew that there was nothing he could say to her. She was not the kind to welcome sympathy from anyone, no less a stranger.

'What do you think will happen, Tom?' Mary asked after a long silence.

'We ain't movin', Mary. We're fightin' if we have to. It looks like tomorrow's the day. I for one have been here too damn long to go somewhere else. I aim to stay right here on my own dirt – or under it.'

The woman's lips sealed tight, and she nodded in complete understanding. Then she looked long into Tom Mahoney eyes, and muttered;

'Be careful, Tom.'

'I aim to be.'

Looking back into the wagon box, she said;

'Are you children all settled in there?'

She waited until she heard three sleepy replies, and then she said;

'Well, wrap up snug in that quilt I left out for you – we're leavin' now.'

The widow took up the reins and slapped them down on the horse's rump.

When Jake returned from the ridge, he simply shook his head.

'You must have somethin' to say,' Tom Mahoney said flatly.

'Not a cloud in the sky, boss. Sorry.'

Mahoney clapped him lightly on the shoulder and said, 'Nobody's blamin' you for the lack of rain, Jake.'

Flinging his arm wide to include the others, he said;

'C'mon, boys. Let's see if we can scare up some grub.'

It was more like trail food than what was usual for a ranch kitchen, but Mahoney and his few remaining hands did not pretend to be cooks.

When the supper was over, the hands drifted off to the bunkhouse and left Mahoney and Halliday to drink the last of the coffee.

After awhile, Mahoney disappeared into the store-room. He returned with a lumpy flour sack, knotted at the neck.

'Here,' he said. 'I may be doin' it hard, but I cain't let you leave with nothin'. Take this for the trail.'

Halliday nodded his thanks and said, 'I guess it's about time I went. It's cool and there's plenty of moonlight. That's about as good as it's gonna get, I suppose.'

'Just remember,' Mahoney said seriously, 'as long as I'm here, you're welcome to come back anytime and stay as long as you want.'

They shook hands without another word, and Halliday went off to get the sorrel. Mahoney lifted a hand in farewell from the porch as Halliday rode out of the yard.

When he was over the ridge, Halliday slowed the horse to a walk. To him at least, there seemed to be the smell of rain in the air. Maybe it wasn't close, but it was there. He could picture it in his mind – powder-dry dirt turning to mud, dry washes suddenly running in a wild flood that eroded the banks, tore trees loose from the ground and carried a burden of writhing snakes and half-drowned prairie dogs on its swirling waters.

He knew where he was heading this time. Before long, he was looking at the lights of Redemption.

EIGHT

ONE STREET
TOO MANY

Late as it was, lamps were still glowing in the bank. Buck Halliday left his horse out front in the near-deserted street and walked around to the back, where he knocked on the door.

After a time, he heard footsteps, and then Finch Rogan opened the door and looked out.

'Hello,' Halliday said quietly. 'You ready to listen now?'

Rogan looked beyond Halliday's shoulder into the darkness, and then shrugged. 'Come in.'

Without looking back to see if Halliday was follow-ing him, Rogan went to his office and sat down behind his desk. When Halliday dropped into the

119

visitor's chair, Rogan looked up at him and shook his head slowly from side to side.

'I figured you'd be gone for good,' he said flatly.

'Could've, except for one thing,' Halliday told him.

'What's that?'

'McPhee is going to start tightening the screws tomorrow, the way I hear it. And the ranchers are goin' to fight him.'

'What's that got to do with me?'

'Just about everything,' Halliday said quietly. 'Even if it wasn't what you meant to happen, you're the man that gave McPhee his chance to squeeze the ranchers out so he can take over Redemption and everything around it.'

Anger flared in Rogan's eyes, and he said;

'All I was trying to do was find some money to keep this town from drying up in the middle of a drought.'

'I know that,' Halliday said, 'but does your backer feel the same? Anybody who didn't know better would think you were in on his plans right up to your neck . . . except for one thing, of course.'

'What's that?' Rogan asked suspiciously.

'You've been shot at twice and wounded once, and at least on the second occasion, the reason was that you were tryin' to organize some more help for Tom Mahoney so McPhee couldn't take his ranch.'

'Dammitall!' Rogan exploded. 'What the hell are

you up to now, Buck? You took my woman and made trouble for me all over town. You killed three men, countin' Rudder, and here you are again – back for more! It's hard to say whose side you're on, but that doesn't seem to matter. Being your friend is every bit as hard as being your enemy. I've had enough. I just want you to get out of here and leave me the hell alone!'

Halliday had never taken that kind of treatment from any man, and even though it was Finch Rogan doing the talking, he found it hard to control his temper.

'I didn't come here to listen to a lot of ranting and raving,' Halliday said tightly.

'So go!' Rogan scowled.

Halliday shook his head.

'When I'm ready and not a minute before. Hell, that woman's sure got her hooks into you, hasn't she?'

'I was going to marry her, and might still do, no thanks to you! I love her. . . .'

'Then you're more of a fool than anybody I've ever met, and if you try to fight about it again, I'll kick you in the butt so hard you won't be able to sit down for a month.'

Halliday stood up and walked across the room, keeping his back to the man. He was giving them both a chance to let their anger subside. This was a touchy business, and he was determined to have it

settled before he rode away. He rolled and lit a cigarette and took a long drag before he turned back to
face the man.

'A man's got to be cautious, Finch,' he said finally.
'That's what you forgot when you got all tangled up
with this town. Just because folks stay put in nice little
houses and don't always carry guns doesn't make it
any different from ridin' a rough trail. McPhee
played you for a fool, and he used Melissa to keep
your brain addled. She's mighty good at what she
does – we both know that.' He paused, drew on the
cigarette again, and said, 'Are you starting to get the
picture?'

'I'm startin' to hate your guts,' Rogan retorted,
'but say your piece. I'm broke and wounded, so you
might as well take the chance to rub my nose in it. It
won't always be like this. One day I'm going to pay
you back for what you've done.'

'OK,' Halliday said wearily. 'At least you're listening, for once. McPhee used Melissa to get to you. All
the time, that little lady was only interested in Wes
Rudder, but she strung you along because McPhee
told her to.'

Rogan opened his mouth to say something, but
Halliday held up his hand and said;

'Let me lay it out for you the way I see it. It's damn
well time you listened. McPhee's made a few mistakes
along the way, but the one that really matters is that
he didn't read people right. Sure, it was easy enough

to push around simple folks, but he tried to treat the ranchers the same way. They're a different breed – we both know that, don't we? Take Tom, for instance. He's willing to die to hold onto what he has. If the drought beats him, he can live with that, but he won't stand for being cheated out of a ranch he's worked so hard to build.'

Halliday stepped forward and leaned on the desk, his forearms bulging with muscle.

'McPhee bought the sheriff and hired a gun hand to keep folks in line. That was bad enough, but for the ranchers, the worst thing he did was to stop them from selling their cattle when they so desperately needed to. He left them with no way out, and they hate him for it. You've seen cattle die of thirst and hunger, and it's not a pretty picture. Making a man watch that happen to his herd is tantamount to slow torture. That's why Mahoney and his neighbors are plannin' to fight. They've got nothing left to lose.'

For the first time, it looked like Halliday's words were starting to sink in.

'They're really going to fight?' Rogan asked.

'And die, if they have to. Can you look me in the eye and say that's no concern of yours, or mine? Think about it, Finch. This country can get along just fine without men like you and me ... but it ain't worth a spit without men like Tom Mahoney and his neighbors.'

Rogan bit his lip and stood up slowly. He raised his

good arm and rubbed the back of his neck.

'Can't see what I can do about it, Buck,' he said slowly.

'You can organize the town, Finch. Tom and his neighbors are all set to fight. If they do it out of town, then I guess they have to accept the consequences. But if they ride in after Harp McPhee, then somebody has got to make sure that Jeff Leonard and his friends know the reason behind it. Otherwise, they're likely to think they have to back McPhee and the sheriff just because Hahn is what passes for law and order in this town. All I want to do before I push on is make sure those towners understand what's happening – that the ranchers' troubles are their troubles. And I think you can help.'

Rogan pursed his lips and fidgeted with his string tie. After a moment's reflection, he nodded and said;

'I'll do what I can. Since you've been doing all this thinking, maybe you can tell me the rest. . . ?'

'Sure,' Halliday said. 'Get the towners together and tell them the whole story. If they don't want to buy into Mahoney's fight, at least make sure they keep right out of it – no matter what Hahn does. That way, the ranchers will stand a chance.'

'All right,' Rogan said grimly. 'Tom will get his chance.'

'That's all we can do,' Halliday said, and then he let himself out the back door and headed straight for the saloon.

He pushed the swing doors apart and walked straight up to the bar, where the sound of a glass breaking was as loud as the crack of doom.

'Damn thing just slipped right out of my hand,' the barkeep muttered.

Heads turned to look at Halliday, but no man uttered a word.

'Whiskey,' Halliday said, and slapped his money down on the counter.

The barkeep served him and hurried away, leaving Halliday alone with empty space all around him.

Halliday took his time, waiting for word of his return to get to Harp McPhee and Luther Hahn.

He didn't have long to wait.

Before the bartender could pour him a second drink, the saloon doors creaked and the subdued buzz of conversation died away again.

Without moving a muscle, Halliday lifted his gaze to the mirror behind the bar.

The barkeep scurried to the little gate at the end of the counter and let himself out. He seemed to have a sudden desire to clean the tables jammed up against the side wall of the saloon.

'You've got some nerve, Halliday,' McPhee said from the doorway.

'Yeah,' Halliday admitted, watching the two men approach the bar.

'What's goin' on in here?' McPhee said loudly. 'Can't a man get a drink anymore?'

'Be right with you,' the barkeep said hastily, but he retreated to the tables again as soon as he had supplied McPhee with a drink from his private stock.

Halliday turned to face McPhee, leaned his elbow on the counter and said quietly;

'Figure you have them where you want them, do you?'

McPhee pursed his lips.

'As a matter of fact, I do. Everythin's turning out just fine,' he said. 'You made a helluva lotta noise, but you were never more than just a nuisance.'

'Why send the girl to seduce me, then?' Halliday asked.

McPhee smiled and shrugged.

'Thought it was a good idea at the time, I guess,' he grinned. 'I wasn't sure how things would go, so I thought it wouldn't hurt to stir up a little trouble between you and Rogan.'

'Your plan nearly worked,' Halliday said.

The first hint of uncertainty showed in McPhee's fleshy face.

'Nearly worked?'

'Finch knows the whole story now,' Halliday said calmly. 'He's even come to realize that Melissa is nothin' but a tramp who does what you tell her to do. I doubt if he can do much to stop you legally, but he's of a mind now to do whatever he can.'

McPhee frowned.

'I'm not exactly shaking in my boots over that

news,' he said. 'I don't see what he can do. Nobody in this town would give him the time of day after he's sold them out. Even if folks would listen to him – and they won't – he can't say I've done anything illegal. I put some pressure on folks, sure, but my business is a tough one. I've lost out before, many times, but this time I'm plannin' to win big.'

'I don't think so,' Halliday said flatly.

'What's that supposed to mean?'

'You'll find out in good time, McPhee,' Halliday told him. 'You spent plenty of time checkin' on ledgers and bank balances, but it strikes me that you fell down by not checkin' up on the people themselves.'

'Like who?' McPhee demanded.

'Tom Mahoney, for instance.'

'Then Tom Mahoney will be ridin' on the wrong side of the law!' McPhee snapped. 'His fight will be with Luther Hahn, not with me. . . .'

Halliday's lips broke into a wide grin.

'Keep talkin' like that, mister, and you might convince yourself even if you don't convince anybody else. The only friends you have in this town are a lawman who you have on your payroll and his wanton daughter. You might have the legal right to take over a lot of businesses and land, but if you try to do it, this town is just goin' to dry up around your ears and leave you with nothing.'

'Who cares?' McPhee said confidently. 'It'll rain some day, and when it does, there'll be plenty of buyers to start it all up again.'

Halliday shrugged.

'I sure don't see how all this is gonna work with nobody but Luther Hahn to back your play – how's his gun hand anyway, still stiff and sore?'

Halliday was surprised to see a spark of amusement appear in McPhee's eyes.

'Who's relyin' on Luther Hahn?' McPhee chuckled. 'He's a good man, but don't think that I'm leaving it all up to him.'

'Far as I know, your hired gun's dead meat,' Halliday said tonelessly.

McPhee could restrain himself no longer.

'Wes Rudder's dead, all right, but now I have his brother. Bob is a better gun than Wes could ever be, and he's goin' to take it personal that you killed his only brother!'

'He'd need to be better than Wes. So when's he due?'

McPhee's knew at once that he should have kept his mouth shut. Without replying, he finished his drink and pushed his bottle back from the edge of the bar. He was turning to leave when Halliday dropped a restraining hand on his shoulder.

'When?' Halliday asked again, and the coldness in his voice sent a shiver down McPhee's spine.

McPhee shook his head.

Halliday released him with a shove.

'Never mind,' he said casually, 'it don't matter. I'll

be waitin' when he comes.'

Now McPhee seemed rooted to the spot, struggling to think of something to say. It was Halliday who left first, sauntering out onto the street as if he were Redemption's favorite son.

Jeff Leonard studied Finch Rogan sourly as the banker followed his wife into the room, and demanded;

'What the hell do you want here?'

'I came to have a talk with you, Jeff,' Rogan said.

'If we ever were on a first – name basis, we sure aren't now.'

Rogan shrugged and dropped his hat on the table. Leonard had just finished his supper, and now he got to his feet.

His wife began to clear the table, and Leonard waited until she had gone off to the kitchen and he could hear the rattle of dishes. He then said;

'I can't imagine what we have to talk about.'

'About the town,' Rogan told him. 'About the ranches that keep this town alive. And about how Harp McPhee has made a fool out of me.'

Leonard's eyebrows shot up in surprise.

'You admit that?'

'I just about have to, don't I?' Rogan replied.

'You sure do, but I never thought you would,' Leonard said. 'We all trusted you, and look where it got us!'

Rogan nodded gratefully as Leonard pointed to a chair and said;

'Well, now you're here, you might as well sit down and say your piece.'

'Tom Mahoney figures I've let him down twice now,' Rogan said. 'I thought I could get him another loan, but the deal fell through. I was counting on the wrong person for help.'

'Who was that?' Leonard asked.

'Melissa Hahn.'

Leonard seemed surprised. He said nothing for a time, and then he asked, 'You know then?'

'I believe I do.'

'Well,' Leonard said carefully, 'I guess it's good to see you've opened your eyes at last. Maybe it's not my place to say it, but a lot of folks figure that girl was two-timin' you. At first, I didn't pay much attention to what they were sayin' – figured they was just jealous. But the more I saw . . .'

'What did you see?' Rogan asked tightly.

Leonard shook his head. 'I'd rather not say.'

'It's best you do. I've already lost a good friend over her, a man I've liked and respected for most of my life.'

The two men looked up when they heard footsteps behind them, and Rogan saw the annoyance in Leonard's expression.

Leonard's wife nodded grimly at Rogan and said;

'I couldn't help overhearing what was just said. I

feel it's only fair to tell you what most of this town already knows. If there was more talk than usual in your case, it's because a banker means something special to a town. Folks look up to men who hole those sort of positions and trust their judgment – or at least that's how it generally goes.'

'So you started worrying how somebody who could be fooled by a pretty woman could be expected to have enough sense to look after your money,' Rogan said flatly.

The woman seemed both embarrassed and relieved.

'Well, yes,' she said. 'Melissa is just no good, and I doubt she has it in her to change.' She hesitated for a moment, and then added, 'There's only one kind of woman who'd hang on to a man like that terrible gunman.'

Leonard gave a despairing sigh and said, 'I think you've said more than enough, Lottie.'

To his surprise, Rogan took the news gracefully, saying only;

'You were right to tell me. Thank you.'

Lottie shot a triumphant look at her husband and left without another word.

After an uncomfortable silence, the storekeeper said;

'Well, what now?'

'Tom is going to fight,' Rogan said. 'I don't know what McPhee will do, but if the fighting spills over into Redemption, I think it's plain what the rest of us should do. It's going to boil down to whether we support the law we voted for, or whether we side with what's right.'

'That's goin' to take some careful thinkin', Finch,' Leonard said.

'People here respect the law out of habit, but if they stop and think, they'll see that in this town, the law has turned against them. Only one man saw through that, and even he was too late.'

'Halliday?' Leonard guessed.

'Yes. If I'd listened to Buck right from the start, I wouldn't be in this mess now.'

'What's Halliday up to now?' Leonard asked as Rogan started down the front steps.

Rogan shrugged and said, 'That's hard to say. One thing's for sure. He's got a perfect right to ride out of here and leave me in the middle of the mess I made for myself.'

Rogan returned to the main street, and as always, his eyes strayed to the bank of which he had once been so proud.

His shoulder was still aching, and he took his arm out of the sling and flexed his muscles to see if it would help.

His mind was filled with thoughts of Melissa and the plans they had made. He remembered lying awake at nights, unable to concentrate on anything because the image of her would not go away. He

132

tightened his lips, realizing that all his dreams were gone now. . . .

Rogan swung toward the bank, but then he paused as he heard the jingle of harness. Melissa drove past without seeing him, and he was close enough to smell her perfume.

She was still a sight to take his breath away, Rogan had to admit. It was not until she had gone from sight that he began to wonder why she was taking the road to Red Rock, all alone and in the dead of night.

Much as he knew it was true, he did not want to believe what he had heard from Buck Halliday and then from Lottie Leonard.

Before he stood up to fight McPhee, he still needed to hear Melissa herself confirm what he knew to be the truth.

Suddenly, his mind was made up. He hurried to the yard behind the bank and saddled his horse.

Rogan had no way of knowing that Halliday had been watching him all along, and was getting his sorrel ready for the trail.

NINE

ONE MAN,
ONE DESTINY

Buck Halliday trailed Finch Rogan all through the night. The sorrel was rested now, but he held it to an easy lope that would overtake neither Rogan nor the girl driving the buggy.

It was in the early hours of the new morning that Halliday rode quietly into the small settlement of Red Rock.

Only the saloon was open, and the light from its windows was the only illumination for the street.

Halliday spotted Rogan's horse hitched down from the saloon, a considerable distance from Melissa Hahn's rig. He chose a different spot, hitching the sorrel to the tie rail outside a millinery store.

He took his time covering the distance to the saloon and kept to the shadows when he got there, so that he could look in through the dusty windows without being seen from the interior.

The saloon was small and narrow, with tables at the back and a curved bar just inside the batwings. A young barkeep was serving a drink to Rogan, who was the only customer at the counter.

There seemed to be a private space beyond the tables, separated from the main room by a curtain, a lamp back there throwing shadows.

Wondering if Melissa was behind that curtain, Halliday walked toward the batwings. He was reaching out to push them apart when he noticed Rogan set down his shot glass and work his bandaged shoulder a little to relieve the stiffness. Halliday saw that Rogan had abandoned the sling he had worn since the shooting, and now he was setting his gunbelt more comfortably on his hip and adjusting the position of the holster.

Something about it all made Halliday remember the time when he had seen his friend take on four men and hold his own. But, of course, those were days when Rogan practiced every day and was not struggling with the stiffness of an injured shoulder.

Rogan was walking away and did not see Halliday enter. The barkeeper raised an eyebrow at the new-comer and held up a bottle, but Halliday shook his head and kept his eyes on Rogan.

He was wondering if he should speak up so Rogan would know he was there, but it appeared that the banker was attempting to talk to Melissa in private.

Something about Halliday's behavior was making the barkeeper nervous – maybe the fact that he had so far refused a drink.

'I sure hope you ain't bent on trouble, stranger,' the young man commented quietly.

'Not unless somebody else starts it,' Halliday replied. 'If anybody does start shootin', you just hit the floor and keep your head down till it's over.'

The barkeeper glanced anxiously toward the curtain at the end of the room. Halliday followed his glance and saw Rogan had paused in front of the covering.

'Who's back there?' Halliday asked quietly. 'Would it be Bob Rudder, by chance?'

The barkeeper's mouth gaped open. He seemed reluctant to answer.

'All you have to say is yes or no,' Halliday told the man softly.

'I think so.'

'Then it might be a good time for you to step outside for a breath of fresh air.'

The barkeeper nodded and started for the door. He stopped twice on the way, apparently meaning to speak, but each time he thought better of it.

Rogan grabbed at the curtain and held it for a moment before he jerked it aside.

Melissa's beautiful, shocked face was the first thing Halliday saw from across the room, but his eyes cut quickly to the three men with her.

'Come on out of there,' Rogan was saying to the girl. 'Whatever you think of me, I just can't let you ruin yourself this way.'

The three seated men scowled up at him, one of them starting to get out of his chair and another setting his glass down so quickly that the contents splashed over his hand.

Even at a distance, Halliday could see that the third man was the dangerous one, a man with an untroubled smirk on his bony face.

'What right have you to follow me like this?' Melissa snapped. 'Get out of here before they kill you like you deserve.'

'You know him then?' asked the man who was obviously the gunman in the bunch.

He rested his hand lightly on the butt of his pistol, and he was leaning forward as if to cover his draw.

'Not by choice,' Melissa said. 'I told you, Bob, I came alone. Mr McPhee wants to see you. He wants to hire you to get the man that killed your brother.'

Rudder glanced at his friends, and then he set his eyes on Finch Rogan, and shifted slightly in his chair. The banker stood his ground and finally said;

'Melissa, I just want to talk to you – that's all.'

The woman picked up her glass, elevated it in Rudder's direction as if she was toasting him, and then threw the stinging contents into Rogan's face.

When he stumbled back blindly, Rudder laughed and made a grab for him. He hit him twice before Rogan was able to raise his fists, but by then the man's companions had him covered with their guns.

Rogan was as surprised as anybody when Halliday said behind him;

'Don't get too hasty, gents.'

The three men turned to study him, and Melissa screamed;

'He's the one, Bob! That's the man who killed Wes!'

'Back off,' the killer said to his two friends. 'This one's mine.'

The only man to move was Finch Rogan, and he made a lunge for Bob Rudder. One of the other two jerked his gun up and fired before anyone knew what was happening.

The bullet took Rogan in the side. As he staggered back, Halliday knocked him to the floor for his own good and fired two shots with nothing more than a split-second between them.

The man who had fired on Rogan snapped back in his chair with blood spurting from the hole in his throat. His companion's head bobbed sharply, his shattered jaw and broken teeth gleaming through the bloody wound in his cheek.

Melissa was screaming on one shrill, continuous note of terror and madness as she cringed and tried to shield herself from the spraying blood. As she threw herself sideways, she knocked Rudder off-balance.

Deliberate as a target-shooter, Halliday lined up his gunsights. The acrid gunsmoke was still thick in the curtained alcove, but Halliday's shot was true, just nicking the lobe of the gunman's right ear.

Rudder clapped his right hand instinctively to his ear, but his left hand shot down to his second six-gun and he fired up at Halliday through the holster, both shots going wide.

Halliday's next bullet tore along the left side of Rudder's face, drawing blood from the ragged gash.

Rudder was cursing as he struggled to get to his feet and draw, but this time Halliday's bullet cut a bloody part in his hair.

Rudder's head flopped back against the wall with a loud thud, the six-gun dropping from his hand.

Melissa had stopped screaming now, and she was looking down at Rudder in white-faced horror. Then she whirled, glaring at Halliday with a snarl of rage that distorted her pretty features.

'All right!' Melissa hissed. 'If none of these fools is good enough to get you, I'll do it myself!'

Halliday started walking slowly toward her. She backed away but caught her foot on the corpse of the throat-shot man who had slid to the floor as the blood pumped from his body. She hit the wall so hard that she let out a gasp and put her hand back to steady herself.

Flinging a chair out of his way, Halliday went to Rogan. When he got close to him, he could see that the man's face was shining with a thin sheen of sweat. The banker looked up at Halliday and said;

'Can you take a look at this? I can't turn around to see how bad it is. . . .'

'Maybe it's not as bad as it feels,' Halliday told him gently.

'Maybe it's worse,' Rogan said with a lopsided grin.

Halliday pulled back Rogan's coat and shirt, mopping the welling blood away with the shirttail.

'I'm no doctor,' Halliday said, 'but it looks to me like the bullet didn't hit any vital organs, pard. If you just set still awhile and let the bleedin' stop, I can get a closer examination.'

Rogan grinned up at him again. He was still holding his six-gun, but now he pressed the heel of his gun hand hard against his side, his hand and the butt of the gun slippery with his own blood.

Halliday tried to lift him into a sitting position. When Rogan's gun bumped against his ribs, he reached down to take it from the wounded man's grasp, but suddenly Rogan twisted and pushed him away with startling strength.

'No, Melissa!' Rogan croaked. 'Don't!'

Halliday turned and saw Melissa standing in her bloodstained clothes, holding a dead man's gun in her shaking fingers.

'Now I'm going to give you something to really remember me by,' she said hoarsely.

Halliday hesitated for just a moment, watching the six-gun waver in her awkward grip.

Then a gun roared beside him, and Rogan groaned and dropped his gun.

At first, Halliday thought that Melissa had fired, but then he saw the young woman begin to fall. She grabbed the side of the table to steady herself for a moment, still clasping the heavy gun. Then she raised her head, and the face that confronted him was no longer the one every man coveted. The blue eyes blazed with madness, the pretty face was full of hate.

She did not have the strength to lift the gun again, but she triggered twice, driving the slugs straight into the tabletop.

Beyond her, Rudder stirred and groaned but did not regain full consciousness.

It was Rogan who dragged himself painfully to Melissa and caught her in his arms as she fell. Then he simply sat on the floor, cradling her body across his knees.

Halliday saw the misery in his eyes.

'Finch,' he said slowly, 'you didn't do it – she did.'

Rogan seemed too dazed to comprehend. While he sat there rocking back and forth, Halliday collected the six-guns that littered the alcove. When he had an armful, he stepped beyond the curtain to find the young barkeeper staring at him, paralyzed with fear.

'I'll have that drink now,' Halliday said. 'Pour one for yourself, too. . . .'

Halliday went behind the building, picking his way carefully in the dark until he found the privy. When he emerged seconds later, the only gun he had was the one on his hip.

When he returned to the bar, he saw that the man on the other side had taken his advice. He dropped some coins on the counter and threw his drink down his throat in one swallow.

'Not bad,' he smiled pleasantly. 'Better than I thought you'd have in a place like this.'

'G-glad you like it, stranger,' the barkeeper faltered.

'You think you could do somethin' for me?' Halliday asked.

The barkeeper nodded dumbly.

'Good. There's a feller in the back room there that's out cold. When he comes to, tell him I've gone to Redemption. What he wants to do about it is up to him. Will you do that for me, friend?'

'S-sure I will, mister,' the barkeeper said huskily.

Halliday heard Rogan calling him then, and he walked back to the alcove behind the curtain. The cramped space smelled of fresh blood and death. He wrinkled his nose in distaste and said;

'Finch, you've gotta get out of here. It's no good

stayin' here like this.'

'Dammit, Buck,' Rogan said in a voice that sounded near exhausted. 'Where the hell are you going now?'

Instead of answering, Halliday said;

'If you can stay out of Rudder's way, I figure Red Rock is as good a place as any for you to spend the next few days. Any fool can see you're in no shape to travel. . . .'

He looked down just once at Melissa's body. It was hard to imagine that night in his room in the boardinghouse. All that silky warmth and wild passion now had become an ugly thing that needed to be hidden from view.

TEN

REDEMPTION

For their own reasons, Harp McPhee and Luther Hahn were both worried men. Nine hours ago, Melissa had gone to Red Rock to fetch Bob Rudder. So far, there was no sign and no word of either Melissa or the gunman.

'Dammit, Luther, we can't just sit here and wonder what's happened,' McPhee insisted. 'Why don't you ride out and look for them?'

Hahn scowled down at his tightly-clasped hands. Ever since sunup, he had the feeling that something was wrong. The last thing he wanted was to have the feeling confirmed.

McPhee kept at him, though. Finally, he nodded and took himself as far as the street door. He was standing there trying to summon whatever it took to go further when all the premonitions started to become fact.

'Mr McPhee,' he said heavily, 'you better come here.'

With the early morning sun behind him, the lone rider was entering town by the trail from Red Rock. It seemed that his horse was following the trail with little guidance from the man in the saddle.

McPhee caught the troubled tone in the sheriff's voice, and hurried to stand beside him. When he saw the rider coming, he frowned and asked;

'Somebody you know?'

'Yeah,' Luther Hahn said, 'that's Bob Rudder, but there's somethin' funny about him.'

'From the way he's sittin' that horse, he looks to be asleep,' McPhee said.

'Yeah. . . .'

'Well, don't just stand there, go talk to him.'

'I don't think we're gonna like what he tells us,' Hahn said honestly.

'So what are you gonna do?' McPhee snapped. 'Hide under your bed or go find out what's happened?'

He gave the sheriff a push and went back into his office to wait. After a time, he heard Hahn's voice from outside.

'You best let me help you down,' the sheriff was saying, and someone else began to cuss.

A few minutes later, a blood-streaked apparition filled the sheriff's doorway, steadying himself against the doorframe as he glared at the man inside.

'Are you McPhee?' the stranger demanded in a hoarse voice.

'I am,' McPhee said carefully. 'Who are you?'

The stranger walked stiffly into the room and stood there with his thumbs hooked in his shell belt, staring at McPhee with an expression that said he wasn't pleased by what he saw.

He was tall and lean, there was dried blood on his face and more of it in his matted hair. He wore all the trappings of a gunfighter and the look of a man who had been allowed to live only because the shame of it would be worse than dying.

'I'm Bob Rudder.'

'I was afraid you'd say that,' McPhee said. 'You look half-dead.' Taking the bottle from the top drawer of his desk, he held it out to the newcomer. 'You better have some of this.'

Rudder accepted the bottle and took a healthy swig. Then he shook a little whiskey into the palm of his hand and rubbed it into his hair.

'I wanna get cleaned up,' he said.

'Luther,' McPhee said, 'show this feller where he can wash up.'

The sheriff led the man out back, and McPhee waited for them to return, his fingers tapping on the desk.

146

Several minutes passed, and then Rudder slouched back into the room and dropped into a chair. The sheriff hovered in the doorway as if he was reluctant to get too close to him. In a way, Rudder looked worse now that the wounds had been bathed. Before McPhee could open his mouth, the gunman began to speak.

'From what I hear, my brother's dead because of the mistakes you made. It ain't gonna be like that with me. I'm gonna be the one that calls the shots from now on. You hear that?'

'Wh-what happened to you?' McPhee stammered.

'A feller by the name of Halliday, is what happened,' Rudder said. 'He got the jump on me in Red Rock. Looked like that woman you sent led him straight to me.'

Rudder picked up the bottle again and took another swig.

Both McPhee and Hahn were wanting to ask him about Melissa, but something in the gunman's manner made them hold their tongues. Finally, Rudder set the bottle down and fixed his eyes on McPhee.

'I want to know exactly what happened to my brother. Come on, spit it out.'

'Halliday got him,' McPhee was quick to say.

'I know that already,' Rudder barked. 'I want to know how.'

McPhee shot a nervous glance at Hahn, who was

edging forward with his hand out for the bottle.

'Stay away from me!' Rudder hissed. 'I heard all about you – the crooked tin star with no guts. Now, who's gonna start talkin'? Maybe you should do the honors . . . *Sheriff.*'

He pronounced the final word as if it was the worst thing anyone could call a man.

Hahn nodded and tried to speak, but the words stuck in his throat. He took a deep breath and started again.

'Wes went after him. It was fair and square, and there was nothin' between 'em when they drew, not a shade. . . .'

Rudder let out a bellow of outrage as he grabbed Hahn by the throat. He pushed him back over the desk with both hands around his throat and held him there, while the sheriff was kicking and struggling helplessly as his face went from red to purple.

It took all McPhee's strength to pull Rudder off, and the gunman immediately turned on him and went for his gun.

'What the hell's wrong with you?' McPhee shouted. 'It ain't our fault your brother's dead. You know who did it, the same man that shot you.'

The gunman went still and stood with his head hanging.

McPhee decided that there would be no better chance to restore his authority, and he jumped at it.

'I asked you to come here to do a job and let you pay Halliday back at the same time for what he did to your brother. Are you interested or not? If you want to work for me, you got to get control of yourself.'

Rudder grunted and let Hahn go.

'Except for Halliday,' McPhee added, 'we got this town sewed up tight. That's why we need you . . . and you need us. It's like Hahn said, your brother called Halliday out and lost. That don't mean to say you have to do the same.'

Rudder glared at McPhee, but finally he wiped the spittle from his lips with the back of his hand and nodded.

Hahn struggled for breath and let out a long sigh of relief, pleased to see that McPhee was back in charge. He coughed and spluttered, then managed to say;

'We need you and you need us. We want Halliday dead, and I just want my little girl back safe and sound.'

'What girl?' Rudder asked sourly.

'Her name's Melissa,' Hahn said quickly.

'Halliday killed her in Red Rock,' Rudder said dismissively.

Hahn stared at the gunman in shocked silence. Then he slumped into a chair and put his hand to his mouth.

'I don't believe it,' he moaned.

'It's true,' Rudder said with little sympathy.

Hahn got up so fast that the chair overturned as he ran for the door.

'Where the hell are you goin', Luther?' McPhee called after him, but Hahn's ears were hearing only one thing, again and again;

'Halliday killed her in Red Rock.'

'Are we talkin' business or not?' Rudder said to McPhee.

'Big business,' McPhee said briskly. 'The way Luther's run out on me, I need you more than ever. You'll have to get some fellers to back you, just in case some gutless townsfolk decide this is their big chance to get brave. Time's runnin' short, but if I hold off foreclosin' on the ranchers for a couple days, that ought to give you time to get settled. I figure it's best if I make myself scarce in the meantime. That all right with you?'

'It's fine by me,' Rudder said. 'But what about Hahn?'

'He could still come in useful,' McPhee said with a sly smile. 'I reckon he's gone to look for Halliday. Why not let him find him? And who knows . . . he might get lucky. It doesn't matter a damn who gets Halliday, just as long as he's got.'

'It matters to me,' Rudder said in a hoarse whisper. 'I want him!'

The sheriff stumbled into the law office like a man in

the grip of a nightmare. He leaned over his desk, supporting himself on the palms of his hands as he stared down at the familiar clutter of Wanted posters and unwashed coffee cups.

The only thing he had ever loved was dead.

It wasn't even a death where men could come up and shake your hand in awkward sympathy and women would leave a basket of food on your doorstep out of kindness. It wasn't that kind of death. Respectable girls don't die in saloons.

Suddenly, it was important to Luther Hahn to know just how and where it had all gone wrong. Melissa had been a good girl by her father's reckoning, wild and full of spirit maybe, but devoted. Hahn first noticed the change in her when she took up with Finch Rogan. Hahn had never liked the banker, but it was clear he worshipped the ground Melissa walked on and he would never do a thing to hurt her.

Rogan wasn't the one to blame, Hahn decided with some reluctance. The simple truth was that the blame rested on Harp McPhee's shoulders.

If it wasn't for McPhee, Melissa would never have become associated with a gunman like Wes Rudder. It was Rudder who lured her into doing things for McPhee, and from there things went downhill fast. Hahn had tried to tell his daughter more than once that she was getting in too deep, but by then, she was hooked.

151

The law office seemed small, cramped and stuffy now. He opened his mouth and gulped in air. Then he wiped his sweating face on his sleeve.

He could not believe that Melissa was dead. He did not want to believe it.

Wes Rudder was not to blame, Hahn admitted. McPhee had been the real architect of all the mistakes Melissa had made.

Then there was Halliday.

Melissa said Halliday had taken her by force in her own room at the boardinghouse, and Rudder said Halliday had killed her in the Red Rock Saloon.

Hahn drew in a quick breath and lifted his head. He stared out the doorway to the street. Everything was quiet. This had been his town. He had walked these streets with pride, and every man showed him respect. The change had come so slowly it was hard to say when decent folks stopped trusting him. He had let McPhee get a toehold, and then a foothold. Now McPhee owned everything in town . . . including the law.

It was hard to say if the words he uttered were a curse or a prayer as Hahn wrenched open the drawer and rummaged through the contents. Finally, he found what he wanted – the linen handkerchief Melissa had embroidered for him when she was still in school. He folded it carefully and tucked it securely into his pocket.

Then he drew his gun and checked the cylinders.

His mind was made up, but even so, he hesitated. He looked around the seedy little office. It wasn't much, but it represented years of his life.

He was going to find Halliday and then settle with McPhee, or he would die trying. It did not matter which way it went, not with his little girl dead.

Bob Rudder didn't enter into his thinking. Sooner or later, he would end up just like his brother.

The sheriff straightened his shoulders and smiled. The planning was complete, and it was a relief to have it done. . . .

Buck Halliday stretched and yawned. The air was stuffy and still in the locked-up bank, and the place had that characteristic smell of all public buildings – ink, brass polish, dust that had lain undisturbed for years in nooks and crannies of the woodwork and plaster, stale cigar smoke.

The clerk had tried to keep him out until opening time, but Halliday had decided the bank was the perfect place to watch and wait. Now he had seen it all – Bob Rudder limping into town like the walking dead, Luther Hahn rushing off to the jail with the look of a desperate man. . . .

Looking over his shoulder, Halliday saw the clerk going about his business as though he was alone. He was counting money into the drawer in the teller's cage now, always the last task to be completed before opening. The minute hand on the big wall clock was edging in tiny increments toward twelve.

'Thanks,' Halliday said quietly. 'I'll leave you to it now.'

The clerk interrupted his counting and looked up.

'You have a good day, Mr Halliday,' he said.

'Always try to.'

Halliday eased open the heavy front door, intending to go to the law office for a word with Luther Hahn. Then he saw Rudder resting against a vacant hitch rail about a hundred yards down from the jail.

Halliday gave the man a wry grin. This was the start of that good day the bank clerk had wished him. Good or otherwise, it was the kind of day he had seen many times before.

He settled his gunbelt just right on his narrow hips and adjusted his hat to shade his eyes from the bright light in the street.

There was no sign of Harp McPhee, who was no doubt playing his usual cautious game. Finch Rogan had not showed up in town, and Halliday hoped that he would stay away. It seemed likely that Tom Mahoney was out on the prairie with his neighbors, preparing to defend their land. That was just how Halliday wanted it. The only way to settle with Rudder was alone.

Quietly closing the heavy bank door, Halliday went down the granite steps and onto the boardwalk below.

He was taking his time, sizing up the distance and

the angle of the morning sun.

When he came to the chosen spot, he stepped into the street, planted his feet firmly and called;

'Rudder!'

The gunman turned and his body stiffened. For one short moment he seemed to hesitate, but then his chest swelled and he moved away from the hitch rail.

'So, you're here,' he snarled.

'Been here awhile,' Halliday said, 'waitin' for you to show yourself.'

Halliday saw Jeff Leonard and two other men coming down the street from the Mercantile. When they saw him and Rudder facing each other, they stopped and backed away.

'You can still walk away if you want to,' Halliday said to Rudder, but the gunman was already going into a crouch.

In a blur of motion, Rudder's right hand dipped down to his holster. He had the gun almost clear of leather when Halliday's bullet took him in the chest and sent him sprawling in the dust of the street.

Rudder knew that he was dying, but he still struggled to lift his gun as he lay on his back. With terrible effort, he tried to level the .45, wanting now to take Halliday with him to hell.

His bony finger tightened on the trigger, but the next bullet came from Halliday and Bob Rudder was as dead as his brother.

Halliday heard footsteps pounding along the street behind him. He spun on his heel to face Luther Hahn. He holstered his gun, but the sheriff kept his in his hand.

'Damn you to hell!' Hahn shouted. 'She was just a girl. Why'd you do it, you son of a bitch?'

'I didn't kill her,' Halliday said flatly. 'And it sure wasn't me who led her astray.'

'Liar!' Hahn roared, and then he fired.

The bullet whistled over Halliday's left shoulder and hammered into the wall behind him.

'If anybody ruined your girl, it was you!' Halliday said coldly. 'She was your own flesh and blood!'

The lawman fired again, missed again, and then Halliday's bullet brought him down.

Halliday simply stood his ground then, watching as Hahn continued to fire until his gun clicked on empty. With the last of his strength, and sobbing with rage and disappointment, Hahn threw the gun at Halliday. Like its bullets, the gun missed its target and fell harmlessly in the dust.

Halliday holstered his gun again and started in the direction of McPhee's office, but before he could get there, a bunch of riders entered the street and reined-in hard just before they reached him.

'You all right, Buck?' Tom Mahoney demanded, but then he saw the bodies in the street beyond him and added, 'Looks like you did fine without us.'

'Wait here,' Halliday told him.

Mahoney had it in his mind to speak again, but something in Halliday's voice stopped him. He waved his companions back and they watched in silence as Halliday walked to the door of Harp McPhee's office and turned the handle. It was locked. He pounded on the panels and waited. Then he drew back one leg and splintered the door with a powerful kick that tore it off its hinges.

McPhee was standing by his desk, cramming papers into a leather bag. All the old arrogance was gone, and McPhee shook with fear.

'You have visitors, McPhee,' Halliday said. 'They're here to talk business.'

McPhee's face was as white as the shirt he wore.

'Everything I did was legal,' he whimpered.

Halliday grabbed him by the scruff of the neck and marched him into the street, releasing him with a hard shove that threw him onto his knees.

With grim deliberation, Mahoney took a coil of rope from his saddle horn and began to fashion a noose.

McPhee saw what the rancher was doing and scrambled to his feet.

'No,' he cried. 'You don't have to kill me to get your lousy town back – I don't want any part of it.'

'Then you're willin' to sign over those mortgages?' Halliday asked.

McPhee spun around to face him, licking his lips nervously. His eyes darted from Halliday to Mahoney as he hesitated, torn between his greed and his fear.

'Let's just try this on for size,' Mahoney said as he approached McPhee with the noose.

Then McPhee saw Finch Rogan pushing his way through the crowd, and he reached out to him desperately.

'Make 'em stop this, Finch!' McPhee begged. 'You know I'm in the right. . . .'

'I don't think so, Harp,' Rogan said calmly. 'I don't believe I know any such thing.'

McPhee's shoulders sagged.

'All right, I'll sign,' he muttered. 'Nobody owes me anything, as of now . . . just so you let me go.'

Halliday stood back, watching with satisfaction as the ranchers frog-marched McPhee back to his office to cancel out their mortgages.

'Halliday?' Jeff Leonard called as he came striding up the street, 'we got somethin' for you. Luther never did it justice. We think you can.'

Halliday looked at the badge in the storekeeper's hand, and then his eyes went to Rogan.

'They're right, pard,' Rogan said with a smile. 'It's about time you tried standin' still for awhile. Redemption has its good points. It really does.'

Halliday shrugged and tossed the badge into the air, firing before it reached the top of its mark but deliberately missing. He caught it as it fell and pinned it to his shirt.

'Must be slowin' down,' he said, but nobody took